FRANK CHRISTIAN—
AGAINST THE CIRCLE R

Frank took Milabel's guns and threw them out the door. Then he overturned the table against the wall in one big heave so there was nothing between them except fifteen feet of clear floor space.

"I made a brag the other night," Frank said. "I'll make another one. I'll pull those leather ears off your thick head and stuff them up your nose, Milabel. And I'm comin' over now."

Milabel lunged across at Frank. Frank stepped inside the swing and shot a hook into Milabel's soft belly. When Milabel jackknifed, Frank raised a shoulder to catch his chin. Milabel's jaw clacked shut and he was straightened up. Then Frank put a flat palm in the man's face and shoved, and Milabel sat down abruptly.

"Hell, stand up," Frank drawled. "I haven't hit you yet."

LUKE SHORT

WAR ON THE CIMARRON

BANTAM BOOKS
TORONTO · NEW YORK · LONDON

*This low-priced Bantam Book
has been completely reset in a type face
designed for easy reading, and was printed
from new plates. It contains the complete
text of the original hard-cover edition.*
NOT ONE WORD HAS BEEN OMITTED.

WAR ON THE CIMARRON
A Bantam Book

PRINTING HISTORY
Serialized in ARGOSY Magazine August-September 1939
under the title HURRICANE RANGE
Doubleday edition published August 1940

*Bantam edition / July 1950
New Bantam edition / August 1959*
2nd printing .. November 1965   3rd printing .... February 1975
4th printing .... December 1980

ISBN 0-553-14183-X

Published simultaneously in the United States and Canada

---

*Bantam Books are published by Bantam Books, Inc. Its trade-
mark, consisting of the words "Bantam Books" and the por-
trayal of a bantam, is Registered in U.S. Patent and Trademark
Office and in other countries. Marca Registrada. Bantam
Books, Inc., 666 Fifth Avenue, New York, New York 10103.*

PRINTED IN THE UNITED STATES OF AMERICA

13 12 11 10 9 8 7 6 5 4

War on the Cimarron

Chapter I

THE SPRING DUSK of the Indian Nations was settling swiftly, and behind him Frank Christian could hear the uneasy bawling of the thirsty trail herd. Here, three days west of the Chisholm and Fort Reno and deep in the Cheyenne-Arapaho reservation's vast grasslands, there were no familiar landmarks, and Frank was as lost as the cattle he was leading. Otey Fleer, sent ahead this afternoon to scout the country and locate Morg Wheelon's place, their destination, was not yet returned; and back on the swing Beach Freeman's young voice, rising in wild curses at the uneasy herd, gave a clue to the temper of the whole crew. Frank stood up in his stirrups to scan the rolling plain again for sight of Otey.

An idle stirring of wind touched his right cheek and lifted the mane of his buckskin gelding, and immediately the situation was taken out of his hands. The lead steer, a mossy-horned old coaster from the Nueces delta, paused in his stride, lifted his head and sniffed the wind and then quartered off to the north at a run. The herd broke then, smelling water, and Frank lifted both hands as a signal to the crew to let them go, and then pulled aside and lifted his horse into a canter. Over to the left the chuck wagon pulled abreast of him and passed him, the horses at a dead gallop, and then the land broke away to show a willow-fringed creek ahead.

In the half dark Frank saw a rider angling up the slope from the creek and he pulled over toward him, letting the cattle stream past on their blind way to water.

Otey Fleer called "Frank?" in the dusk, and Frank answered and they met.

"Was this shack of Morg's set on the hairpin bend in the creek, with a stand of live oaks behind it?"

"That's what Morg wrote. Where is he?"

"I never went up," Otey said. "I figgered to come back and catch you before dark."

"How far is it?"

1

"Four-five miles. I reckon we better bed down the herd here and not try to make it," Otey said.

Frank looked sharply at his *segundo*, sensing the caution and lack of enthusiasm in his voice, and then pulled his horse around and headed for the creek and the fire that was already built beside the chuck wagon.

Samse Benson, the horse wrangler, already had his rope corral built for the night herder's mounts, and the rest of the crew of four men was drifting wearily toward the campfire and late supper.

They were waiting the word to offsaddle when Frank rode in among them. Seen in this dusk, he was unmistakably Texan, tall and bleach eyed and narrow hipped. Without dismounting he leaned wearily on his saddle horn, thumb-prodded his Stetson back off his forehead and scrubbed a lean, browned and beard-stubbled jaw with the flat of his hand. His glance was directed at the cattle beyond, who had tramped down the willows in their thirst and crowded the creek on both banks. He seemed to concur with Otey's opinion and called to the horse wrangler. "Turn out the whole remuda, Samse. No night herdin' tonight. We're on home ground."

A whoop of joy lifted to the lowering night sky, and Frank Christian suddenly grinned. Immediately he seemed younger than his twenty-seven years. There was a kind of rash and friendly derisiveness in his gray eyes as he laughed at the relief of his crew, for the drive had been a long and hard one. But when he caught sight of Otey Fleer, still mounted, utterly silent, his grin faded and was replaced by a troubled frown. Beach Freeman, youngest man in the crew, walked over to him and said, "You ain't hoorawin' us, Frank? This is really home ground?"

"You'd be ridin' night herd, all right, if it wasn't."

"I just wondered," Beach said. "I choused thirty head of strange beef away from the creek tonight."

A scowl creased Frank's forehead for a moment, and then he pulled his horse around. "I'm headin' for Morg's shack tonight, Beach. Bring the horses and the wagon up the creek to the shack tomorrow, and day after we'll scatter the herd."

Afterward he rode over to Otey and said, "You come with me, Otey," and his *segundo* pulled in alongside him and they rode out of the faint circle of firelight. Otey was a wry little man, wrinkled and unshaven and untidy and profane, and seldom given to enthusiasms. But in all the years he had punched cattle in Texas Otey had never seen grass like this, and Frank was irritated at his silence. He asked presently, "How does it look, Otey?"

"Oh, the range looks all right," Otey said grudgingly.

Frank looked over at him, but coming darkness hid the little man's face. "Well, what don't you like about the rest of it?"

Otey said sulkily, after a minute's pause, "Nothin'," and they lapsed into silence. This creek, Paymaster by name, was a landmark in his life, Frank thought—the end of one part of his life and the beginning of another. Morg Wheelon, his partner, was waiting for him at the shack up ahead, and the prospect of that meeting gave him a small excitement.

Last year he and Morg had thrown in together as partners, pooling all the money they had earned as trail bosses and all they could borrow in Texas. That money had gone toward a scheme that most men thought fantastic. The Chisholm Trail, when it left Texas, passed successively through the Comanche-Kiowa, the Cheyenne-Arapaho and the Cherokee reservations, the vast land of the Indian Nations that stretched from Kansas to Texas and had a "no trespassing" sign on it for white settlers. It was a country filled with not-too-friendly Indians policed by the U.S. Army and with outlaws wanted in every state and territory of the West; but above and beyond that, it had grass belly deep to a horse. A few hardy cattlemen, incorporated into companies, had come onto the reservations and had leased hundreds of thousands of acres from the Indians. On these acres, which they protected by the sheer toughness and size of their crews, they wintered their herds of Texas beef and sold them at top prices at the near markets in Dodge City and Caldwell. It was no place for the small rancher, cattlemen opined. The big companies didn't need sheriffs, juries, jails and the protection of the law; they were their own law. The little rancher, on the other hand, didn't have a chance. And Morg Wheelon and Frank didn't agree.

Morg had stayed in the Nations this past winter while Frank went back to Texas to scrape together a trail herd. Two months ago Morg had written that he had leased fifty thousand acres on the Cheyenne-Arapaho reservation from the Cheyenne chiefs, had built a shack and corrals and was waiting for the herd. Tonight, then, they were ready to begin proving that the Nations was a country for little men too.

Interrupting his own reverie, Frank said, "Otey, wait till you see what our herd looks like next fall."

"I wisht I could," Otey said sourly.

"Why won't you?" Frank said.

"It don't look like I'd be here."

Frank didn't speak for a moment, and Otey said in sulky distaste, "Dammit, Frank, you and Morg should have got together better on what you planned."

"Why's that?" Frank asked.

Otey looked at him in the darkness. "When you hired me you told me I was to stay on as foreman of the crew on the lease here, didn't you?"

"That's right."

"You told them other boys—cook, Samse, Beach, Phil and Mitch—that they was hired permanent, didn't you?"

"That's right. They are."

"Then what's Morg doin' with a crew a'ready?"

Frank glanced swiftly at him, but it was too dark to see the small man's face. He pulled up his horse and Otey pulled his up, and Frank said quietly, "What are you talkin' about?"

"Morg's hired a crew," Otey said positively. "Even down to the cook. I counted eight men at that shack, besides the cook."

"I thought you didn't go up."

"I never. When I come in sight of it there was five men and a hell of a lot of horses in the pasture. I took a pasear back into the live oaks and watched the house, and I'm tellin' you, Frank, I counted eight men and a cook!"

"Morg never hired them, I know. He wrote me to bring the crew."

"Them riders belonged there," Otey said bluntly. "They wasn't just stoppin' off to pass the time of day."

Frank didn't say anything but put his horse into motion. Presently Otey said, "All day long ridin' the creek I been seein' cattle that don't carry a brand you or Morg ever registered anywheres."

Frank said in sharp disgust, "Hell, Otey, you're spotted the wrong place, I reckon."

"Frank, pull up. I want to talk to you," Otey said.

There was an urgency in his voice that made Frank obey. Otey went on in his tough, wry voice, "You know and I know that we've followed Morg's directions from Fort Reno. We've hit the right creeks, we've seen the right landmarks, and this here creek is Paymaster Creek. We've passed that red limestone outcrop that Morg wrote about, and that shack is in a hairpin bend of the creek. And just to make sure I took a

pasear over to the north and spotted them salt licks that Morg
wrote about. I got the right place. Now you tell me what
Morg is doin' with strange cattle on your range and a crew
to punch 'em."

Frank said quietly, "Let's find out," and moved on. Otey
didn't say anything. They forded the creek at a place he had
picked out that afternoon and followed the creek on the other
side until it swung abruptly north. And then, up the gentle
slope, a small pin point of light appeared.

"There's the bend and there's the light," Otey said.

They rode on, turning up the slope. Presently they had to
detour for a pasture fence, and then they were beside the
corrals. Frank rode straight on toward the house. When he
was a hundred feet or so from it the lamp suddenly winked
out inside, and a voice from under the dark gloom of the
porch said, "Sing out, boys!"

Frank pulled his horse to a stop. "Where's Morg?"

There was a long pause. "Morg who?"

"Morg Wheelon. This is his place."

"Who's talkin'?" the voice asked.

Frank's voice took on an edge. "Mister, I'm comin' over
there, and I'm comin' peaceable. I want to talk."

He dismounted and walked slowly toward the house. He
heard the man on the porch say softly, "Light the lamp,
Chet," and then say to him, "Wait'll there's light, and then
come slow, both of you."

A match flared and then the steady glow of the lamp replaced it, and Frank walked onto the porch and paused in the
doorway. Five riders had been interrupted in their game of
cards. They stood around a big table that filled the center of
a bunk-lined room. The light from the lamp brought out the
sharp planes of their suspicious faces, and Frank picked out
the biggest man and said, "Where's Morg Wheelon?"

This man shifted his feet gently and rammed both thumbs
in the waistband of worn levis. He was a huge man, heavy
and tall, with a thin saddle of sandy hair across his nearly
bald head, and he had a broad, hard-bitten face that was
utterly placid in front of deep-set alert eyes.

"Morg Wheelon?" he murmured. "Don't recollect the
name. This is a line camp of the Reservation Cattle Company, though."

Frank stepped slowly into the room. He might have been
an ordinary puncher, for his clothes—checked cotton shirt,
faded levis, black silk neckerchief, dust-colored Stetson and

scuffed half boots—were common enough for Texas men. But there was something in his big-boned six feet of height and in his slow-moving manner that told of authority. He looked carefully about the room, at the cluttered gear on the dirt floor, at the ten bunks piled with blankets and clothes, at the door that let out to the cook's lean-to.

His gaze finally settled on a group of pictures cut out of magazines that was pasted on the log wall over a single bunk. A hunch prompted him to stroll across the room and examine the pictures. One was a drawing of a pacing horse, tail out, mane streaming and feet daintily lifted.

Frank turned slowly to the five men and then nodded at the pictures. "Who owns them?"

"I do," the heavy man said.

"Nice picture of a horse. What horse is it?"

"I dunno. I just cut it out."

Frank said evenly, "You're a liar. That's a picture of a pacer, Lady St Clair, from San Francisco. She made a record for five miles at Frisco in seventy-four, and Morg saw her do it. I've looked at it a hundred times. That's Morg's picture and he pasted it there." His gray eyes were suddenly sultry, and his glance bored at the big man. "Where's Morg?"

The man in the doorway, gun still trained on Otey's back, said, "Don't talk, boss."

"I got nothin' to hide," the heavy man said firmly, his glance fixed on Frank. "Morg Wheelon is dead."

There was a long, long pause.

"Dead?" Frank echoed blankly.

"That's right. Talk to Major Corning in Fort Reno. The army investigated it. About three weeks ago one of my riders called in here to pass the time of day, and Morg was lyin' in the yard by the horse corral. Somebody had fist-fought him and then let him have it with a load of buckshot."

After another long pause Frank said, "And you're who?"

"Chet Milabel. I'm foreman for the Reservation Cattle Company."

"And what are you doin' in Morg's place here?"

Milabel shook his head slowly. "It ain't Morg's place. After he was murdered the company leased this chunk of land from the Cheyennes. We paid good hard money for it too. This shack was on the lease, so we moved in."

Frank shuttled his glance to Otey, whose face was stiff with dismay, and then he looked back at Milabel.

"There's only one thing wrong with the way that shirt

hangs, Milabel. Morg Wheelon had a partner, and I'm that partner."

Interest quickened in the foreman's eyes. He studied Frank with a careful unhaste and then said, "I'd want proof of that before I believed it, and it wouldn't change things much if I did believe it."

"You're goin' to believe it. You're goin' to hear Chief Stone Bull tell you—after I've moved you out of here."

A slow smile broke Milabel's heavy face. He shook his head and murmured, "You're green to these Indian politics, I can see." He gestured to a bunk. "Sit down."

"No."

Milabel spread his legs a little wider and rocked back on his heels. He talked now with a slow and wicked relish. "There ain't anybody going to help you. All a man has to do to lease graze on this reservation is to hunt up ten Indians, any ten Indians, and give 'em some money. Then he squats on a piece of land and holds it if he can. That's what Morg Wheelon did. He hunted up Stone Bull, an old chief and a good one, and give him some money and then picked this piece. But I can hunt up four other chiefs who'll say they never saw the color of Morg Wheelon's money. And I can hunt up a dozen white men, whisky peddlers to the Indians, who claim to be lease agents for the Indians, and they'll say Morg Wheelon didn't pay them." He shook his head slowly. "You ain't got any claim on this land, my friend—not unless you got plenty men with guns behind you to back it up. Have you?"

"I don't reckon," Frank said, studying each man's face, "I don't reckon I'll need that many."

"I wouldn't try it with less," Milabel murmured.

"I'll try it." Frank hitched up his levis. "I'll give you a week to pull off this lease. Move your cattle and your gear. No, I'll give you two days, just forty-eight hours. I don't like your face."

Milabel's faint smile vanished, and Frank went on in a low, wicked voice, "There's just one thing I want out of you, Milabel. Who killed Morg Wheelon?"

"I know the Reservation Cattle Company didn't, and that's all I care."

Frank said, "After I kick you off this place I'm goin' to find out if that's so."

The man in the door swore softly, and at the sound of his voice Milabel stirred himself and tramped slowly across to

Frank and hauled up facing him. He said gently, "You talk
like a hard case. Are you one?" and suddenly drove his fist
into Frank's face. Frank tried to dodge, and the blow skidded
along his jaw, but there was force enough in it to send his
head back against the wall with a sharp and savage rap that
about split his skull.

His knees hinged and he sat down loosely on the floor, and
Otey's hand made only the faintest flicker of a movement toward his gun before he felt a gun barrel rammed in his back.

Otey said bitterly, "You'll be sorry for that, Milabel."

"Tote him out of here and keep him out," Milabel said.

Otey walked over to Frank and stood him on his feet and
then ducked under his arm and half dragged, half walked
him out into the night.

When he reached his horse he felt Frank take up some of
his slack weight, and Otey put Frank's hands on the saddle
horn. For a half minute, perhaps, Otey held him there, and
then Frank took his weight and shook his head slowly from
side to side.

When he raised it he looked around him and then over
his shoulder at the house. He shoved away from the horse,
striding toward the light.

Otey grabbed him roughly and swung him around. "Stay
out of there, Frank!"

Frank wrenched his hand free and swung up his gun and
started again, and then Otey knew he would have to do it.
He whipped up his gun and brought it arcing against Frank's
head, and then Otey caught him as he was falling on his face.

Afterward Otey loaded him across the saddle and led his
horse toward the creek and their camp.

Chapter II

WITH HIS SELF-IMPOSED DEADLINE less than two days away
there were a lot of things Frank had to do and do quickly, and
when he rode into Fort Reno the next noon there was naked
temper in his gray eyes. One of those things was to find out
what he could about Morg's death. This morning he had
remembered a line in Morg's last letter to him. Morg had said
that if everything went right for them during the coming year

there was a girl at the agency, Edith Fairing by name, whom he was going to marry. She was the one to see first.

But with a couple of small errands to do first Frank rode into the garrison. Fort Reno was located at the crown of a long grassy slope that lifted from the banks of the north fork of the Canadian River. Across the wide sandy river bed of the Canadian lay Darlington, the agency town of the Cheyenne-Arapaho reservation. Garrison and agency were in sight of each other, perhaps a mile apart. Frank was familiar with the garrison, for it was a supply point for trail-herd commissaries as they passed up the Chisholm Trail miles to the east. The garrison buildings lay on the four sides of the long bare rectangle that was the parade grounds, and this year, 1883, the barracks were of stone and there were sidewalks and young trees and even street lamps.

Frank swung into the drive that circled the parade grounds and headed toward the sutler's post, the garrison trading center. On the northeast corner of the parade grounds it reared up in two-story wooden vastness, a huge building that held a big store, a saloon, a restaurant and a barbershop on the first floor, with a hotel on the second floor. It was flanked by a fenced wagon yard, feed stable and blacksmith shop, and the whole building was the center of life at the post.

Passing the long wooden-awninged porch that crossed the entire front of the building, he was aware of the curious stares of the two dozen loafers, blue-coated troopers and Indians and punchers who congregated there. In the big wagon yard next door to the hotel there were a half-dozen freighting outfits making up for the trip to Caldwell, Kansas, a hundred and fifty miles to the north. And among these massive wagons there was one dainty buggy with bright red wheels, and it was pulled up in front of the office which bore the legend: HAY AND FEED, LIVERY RIGS FOR HIRE.

Frank dismounted and, squinting against the bright spring sun, stepped into the dark office. Immediately he was aware of a woman's voice saying, "—and six sacks of corn. Dad wants to know if you can get it right away, because they'll deliver to the quartermaster tomorrow. If you can't, they'll bring their remuda here."

"Sit down, Miss Barnes. Sit down," a man's voice said. "Jake Humphries ain't workin'. I'll see if he'll freight it out."

The sun glare washed out of Frank's eyes, and he caught only the briefest glimpse of a girl in a blue print dress walking toward a chair. The clerk, a bald man in shirt sleeves wearing iron-rimmed glasses, stepped toward the door and, seeing Frank, stopped and said, "What'll you have, mister?"

"I want a load of corn freighted out to my place."

The clerk went back to the desk and picked up a pencil. "What name?"

Frank told him, and the clerk said, "And where to?"

"On Paymaster Creek. Pick up the creek at Turkey Ford and follow it to the first hairpin bend."

The clerk raised his head abruptly. "Ain't that the Circle R line camp?"

"It was," Frank said.

"You bought it?"

"It's mine," Frank said, a hint of temper in his voice. "They're movin'."

"Will they help you freight it?" the clerk continued.

Frank looked puzzled. "Help? Why should they? I'm buyin' the corn and you're freightin' it."

The clerk shook his head patiently. "Christian, I ain't freightin' any corn out there unless the Circle R is guardin'. If I tried, it would never get there."

Frank's deceptively mild gaze studied the clerk for a moment. "Be plain," he said.

"All right," said the clerk. "Who'd you lease your range from?"

"The Indians."

"Sure. Which ones?"

"Stone Bull got the lease money," Frank said, puzzled.

The clerk shook his head and threw down the pencil. "Understand, this is just an observation of mine," he said, "but I've noticed that if a man leases Indian land from Scott Corb, he never has trouble with his freightin'. If he don't lease it from Corb, he does. The Circle R didn't lease from Corb, and they have to throw a guard around every wagon that leaves here." He paused and shrugged. "If I sent a wagon out, it would be wrecked, my teamster beat up and the corn burned."

"So that's the word," Frank said.

"That's it. I'm sorry, but you don't get no corn unless you supply the wagon and guards and pay cash for the freight." He stepped around Frank and walked out into the bustling yard yelling for Jake.

Frank was suddenly aware that the girl was looking at him from her chair in the corner beside the desk. She was a slim girl with a mass of wheat-colored hair pinned in a loose knot at the base of her neck. There was a repose in her face now that was broken by a faint smile on her full lips. Her wide-set blue eyes were curious as they regarded Frank, and then when he looked at her she dropped her gaze.

Frank pulled off his Stetson, revealed a head of thick dark hair that was not carefully combed and walked over to her. "I couldn't help but hear you," he began. "Didn't you order corn?"

"Why—yes."

"And do you lease from this Corb?"

"My father's a beef contractor to the Indians and the army," she explained in a low voice. "We don't lease from anybody."

Frank, still puzzled, nodded his head toward the door. "Was that straight, what he told me?"

"I'm afraid it is."

Frank didn't say anything for a long moment, looking at her. He was remembering what Chet Milabel had told him last night, and then he said meagerly, "This Corb couldn't be a whisky peddler, could he?"

Involuntarily the girl started, and then she said swiftly, "It's never been proven. Corb is the informal lease agent for a good part of the Cheyennes. This freighting business is just —well, a way he has of making cattlemen want to lease from him."

Frank drawled softly, "I reckon it's about time he changed his ways."

The girl smiled suddenly, and there was pity in the smile. "You're not the first man who thought that."

"Where are the others?" Frank asked.

"They don't run cattle here any more."

Frank grinned suddenly. "They didn't make big enough tracks, is that it?"

The girl's smile faded. "I wouldn't say that. They were just—well, bullheaded."

"Like I'm goin' to be?" Frank asked.

The girl nodded. "And I wouldn't be, if I were you."

The clerk came in then and announced that Jake Humphries would take care of the freight, and the girl went out without a backward glance. She climbed into the buggy and drove out of the compound, and Frank watched her thoughtfully, a new anger stirring within him. Apparently leasing on the Cheyenne-Arapaho reservation was a question of politics besides a question of murder.

He rode out past the hotel and, catching sight of the sutler's bar in the corner of the building, was reminded of his headache, which was throbbing with every beat of his heart. A glass of whisky might knock it, he reflected, and he dismounted and went inside. There was a scattering of civilians and army officers inside, and he bellied up to an empty space in the bar and called for a whisky.

As the bartender laid the bottle on the counter Frank heard someone say, "Christian?"

He turned to regard a man who had come up beside him yet had kept a small distance between them, leaning both elbows on the bar. He was a colorless-looking man, thin, of average height and dressed in a careless black suit whose trouser legs were thrust into scuffed half boots. His face was sallow, strong muscled, and his mouth was half hidden by a thin and ragged mustache of an indeterminate roan color. It was his eyes, however, that made the man jell and pushed his character into the open, for they were black and shiny as obsidian, their alertness veiled by sleepy lids.

"Yes," Frank said.

"I'm Scott Corb." He made no effort to shake hands, as if he knew it would be a pleasure to neither of them.

"Yes," Frank said again, interest in his voice now.

"Morgan Wheelon was your partner, wasn't he?" When Frank nodded Corb went on.

"He overlooked somethin' before he died. You might like to straighten it out."

"What's that?"

"He never paid for your lease," Corb said.

Frank smiled faintly. "Paid you, you mean."

"That's right. I'm the lease agent for about three quarters of these Cheyenne and Arapaho. Wheelon gave some money to a small chief, and it's the opinion of the council that you'll be squattin' on their land if you take over."

Frank looked beyond him to the two riders back of Corb who were listening, studying the back bar mirror with a show of boredom. His glance shuttled to the mirror, and he saw at a table behind him a man who had not been there when he entered. He knew the signs well enough, knew that Corb had arranged this to take care of any trouble.

He scrubbed his jawline with the flat of his palm and said mildly, "I been tryin' to get corn today, Corb. You throw that in too?"

"If you pay for your lease," Corb said.

The men in the room were quiet, listening, knowing what was happening and waiting for Frank to make his decision.

Slowly he reached out for the bottle of whisky, seemed to fumble it and contrived to spill it on the bar top, neck toward Corb. The whisky gurgled out, and Corb leaped away from the bar, lifting his arms up. But it had been too quick for him, and when he lowered his arms a thin stream of whisky streamed from his coat sleeves. He raised his rash and wicked glance to Frank's face, and small spots of color appeared on his sallow cheeks.

"Why damn me for a fumble-fingered fool!"" Frank said mildly. "Why'd I do that?" His cold gaze rose to Corb's and he'd it.

For a split second Corb hesitated and then, willing to give Frank a chance, said, "Accident."

Frank smiled crookedly. "It wasn't any accident, Corb. If you want to be paid for that lease, wring out your coat sleeve in a glass and I'll pay the barkeep for it. That's the only money of mine you'll ever see."

He laid a coin on the counter, wheeled and walked indolently out the door, and behind him the room was utterly silent.

Mounted again, he rode out of the garrison toward the agency across the river, his anger still hot. Corb's oblique threat was still in his mind, and he didn't care now. It looked as if his lease was going to be a three-cornered battleground, with Morg's killing the first move on somebody's part. To his suspicion of Milabel he quietly added the name of Corb, remembering what the girl in the feed office had said.

Down the slope past the issue corrals he put his horse into the wide river bed of the Canadian and heard a team behind him. He pulled out of the rutted tracks, not even looking around, and then he saw the red-wheeled buggy pull up abreast him and heard a man say "Whoa," and he stopped.

There was the girl, all right, on the other side of the buggy, and holding the reins was a man of huge girth and a pleasant red face which was perspiring. The big man put out his hand and said, "I was in the sutler's bar when you done it, Christian. I'd like to shake your hand."

Frank, puzzled, shook hands with him, and the big man said his name was Hopewell Barnes. "And this is my daughter, Luvie."

"We've met," Luvie said. There was a disapproving look in her face, but Barnes went on. "That's somethin' I see all too seldom—a man stand up to Corb."

"So I heard," Frank drawled, looking at Luvie, and her cheeks colored.

Barnes wiped his face with a big bandanna and then said, "Luvie told me about meetin' you. She said you needed corn."

Frank nodded. "I came in off the trail yesterday with my remuda gaunted up. Looks like I'm goin' to have to feed 'em up on grass, though."

"No, you ain't. Just suppose a load of corn I ordered got misdirected to your place, and you started usin' it before I found out?"

Frank studied him briefly, then grinned. "I'd sure hate that. I'd have to pay for it and let it go at that."

"Dad, be careful!" Luvie said swiftly. "Corb will see through that."

Barnes turned to her, frowning. "No, he won't. It's legal."

"But this man has quarreled with him already! He's sure to!"

Frank leaned both hands on the saddle horn, and impatience touched his voice. "You never finished tellin' me about Corb, Miss Barnes. Go ahead, now that there's nobody can hear."

Luvie's eyes flashed, but before she could retort Barnes said, "It's somethin' you'll find out, Christian. I can tell you this. The Circle R is the only outfit on the reservation that can fight him. The rest can't, me included. His business, you see, is to hire a bunch of Texas hard cases. They buy whisky in Kansas, freight it down to their caches here in the Nations and use it for money. Outfits come in, like you, and want to lease range. If they lease from Corb, he takes their money and pays the Indians off in whisky. If they don't lease from him, he makes life purely hell for them."

"And he will for you!" Luvie said.

Frank's glance shifted from her to Barnes. "Maybe you'd better not get mixed up with it then, Barnes. I'll make out without the corn."

"No!" Barnes roared. "I don't have a crew, and I can't fight Corb. But I'm willin' to help any man that will fight him!" He shook out his reins and glared at Frank. "The offer still holds. You want the corn?"

"Obliged," Frank said. "I do." He touched his hat and Barnes drove away, but not before Frank saw Luvie lean across toward her father and begin to talk to him in a low, animated voice.

Thoughtfully Frank rode into Darlington in the early evening light. It was a small town, a hotel and a scattering of stores facing a wide street. Indians loafed on the sidewalks and in the street and stared impassively at Frank as he dismounted in front of a restaurant. He ate a lone meal and afterward found out from the waiter that Edith Fairing, the daughter of an agency employee who had died last year, lived in a small house down the next street east.

Afterward, following directions, Frank dismounted in front of the place. It was full dusk now, and he could not see a light in the house but he went up the walk.

Somebody rose out of the swing, and, coming closer, Frank saw it was a girl. She was a dark-haired pretty girl with grief still in her eyes, and when Frank introduced himself she smiled a little and invited him to sit beside her in the swing.

"I—just heard about Morg last night," Frank began.

"I'd have written you, Frank, but I didn't know where you were. It happened three weeks ago."

"It won't bring Morg back, but somebody is goin' to pay for that," Frank said softly, vehemently.

"Nobody will pay for it," Edith said bitterly. "That's what's so awful."

Frank looked at her sad face in the fading light. "I come to you for help. I'm not goin' to take this lyin' down. I want to know what you can tell me."

"Nothing."

"Somebody killed him," Frank insisted.

Edith turned her head toward him then, and there was a wry bitterness in her voice as she spoke. "I've thought of that. Any number of people could have killed him, for any number of reasons!"

"Name some."

"The Reservation Cattle Company. Your lease lies between two of theirs. If they're to fence and protect their lease, they must have yours."

Frank nodded slowly. "That's one. What's another?"

"Scott Corb has a way of making people regret it if they don't lease from him."

"All right," Frank said in a low voice.

"There's a hundred young Cheyenne bucks on this reservation who hate the white men. They're inciting the others to war. Only the old chiefs keep them from an open war."

"A hundred Indians," Frank said grimly. "Who else?"

"Half the wanted men in the West are hiding out in the Nations, Frank. They'll kill a man for a handful of matches!"

Frank was silent, baffled. It was true. He felt Edith stir beside him, and he looked over to find her crying quietly in her handkerchief. It was the sick, sobbing grief of a woman in despair, and Frank felt a pity for her and was helpless to comfort her.

Edith rose suddenly, and Frank came to his feet. "I—can't talk about it, Frank. You—better go."

"I'll come back tomorrow then," Frank said.

Edith laid a hand on his arm and her fingers were tense. "I didn't mean that, Frank. I meant you had better leave the country! Get out! Give it up! They'll get you too!"

And before Frank could answer she brushed past him and disappeared in the house. Frank stood there a moment, feeling anger flood him anew and tighten every muscle in his body.

Afterward he went out to his horse and mounted and took the road to the garrison again. Everywhere he had turned this day there was fear and dread and hopelessness. He had seen it everywhere, from the time he entered the feed office to this moment. And still he knew nothing about Morg's death. Crossing the river, he knew there was only one source of information left to him, and that was the army. He would stay the night at the garrison hotel, and early in the morning he would closet himself with the major in command and learn everything that was known about Morg's death.

At the garrison he rode past the porch of the sutler's post and into the wagon yard. By the light of the lantern hung beside the feed-office door he saw that the yard was cleared of freight wagons and the black depths of the open-faced wagon sheds on two sides of the compound were dark and deserted. He rode on through to the stable archway ahead and it was dark. Through its long driveway and out by the corral he saw that a lantern had been left for the late riders. He turned his horse into the corral and then came back through the stable to the compound.

As he stepped out of the stable into the wagon yard he was aware of something changed. For a moment in the dark he was puzzled, and then he knew. Someone had doused the lantern hanging beside the feed-office doorway since he rode through a moment ago.

Frank came to a halt, feeling his nerves screw tight. The deep wagon shelters lay ranked on each side of him, darker than the night. To reach the faintly lighted street beyond the compound gate he would have to walk past these wagon sheds.

A cold uneasiness coiled inside him and he fought it down. The stable hostler probably hadn't heard him and had doused the lantern.

Just then a man afoot swung through the compound gate ahead. He was whistling a thin cheery tune faintly off key.

Frank walked on and had taken a dozen steps when he heard a voice call from one of the wagon sheds, "Christian?"

He stopped dead, and before he turned his head to look in that direction he noticed that the man who had come through the gate also stopped.

He didn't answer. Another voice from the other side of the compound called, "All right."

Then a shot broke the night. It came from the direction of the first voice, and the slug rapped into the claboard of the stable.

Palming his gun up, the salt taste of anger in his mouth, Frank ran in the direction of the second voice, the closest, and the angry purple-orange flare of a gun blossomed high under the wagon shed.

Frank whipped up his gun and, running, shot at it and he heard a man curse under the uneasy stomping of a nervous horse. He shot again, and the hidden man across the compound shot too, and then the man up by the gate yelled: "Get under that wagon shed, Christian!"

The man across the compound threw a shot in the direction of the gate, and then Frank pounded into the dark shadows of the shed and flattened himself against the back wall. He listened to the man up ahead fight his horse, and he shot once and his fire was not returned.

Suddenly the man across the compound broke away from the shadows. He was mounted and he was riding straight across to join his partner.

Frank swung his gun up, but before he could shoot, two shots in rapid succession came from the man by the gate. The horse swerved and grunted and went down, and its rider catapulted over its head. He scrambled out of the dust then and crawled behind the down horse and yelled miserably, "Get out the back way, you damn fool!"

The other rider put his horse out from the shed at a dead run, heading for the stable archway, and the man afoot wheeled and ran in the same direction. In that uncertain light Frank emptied his gun and saw them both vanish in the archway.

Almost immediately he heard the noise of men on the

street running toward the stable. Then out of the darkness the lone figure of a man appeared. He stopped and said, "Christian?"

It was the man by the gate.

Frank said, "All right."

"Keep your mouth shut and let me talk," the man said.

And Frank walked up to join him and face the crowd which was coming through the gate.

As soon as the lantern was lighted a blue-uniformed army captain took command. He came striding toward Frank and the stranger, who was standing just beyond the downed horse.

"What's going on here?" the captain asked in a voice of iron authority.

Frank glanced obliquely at his companion. He was an unshaven and redheaded young puncher in ragged clothes, and his face, pleasantly homely, was overlaid with a tough and amused defiance that did not change at the sight of authority. He was a solid man, inches shorter than Frank, and his shirt was so ragged that patches of sunburned skin showed through the rents in his sleeve.

The captain was a small man with a cavalryman's stiff gait. When he saw Frank's companion he stopped and said sourly, "Oh. You again."

"That's right," the redhead said.

"What was all the shooting about?"

The redhead let the curious crowd of garrison loafers form a loose circle about them, and then he gestured to the downed horse. "I come in here for my horse. Soon's I stepped in the gate all hell broke loose. A couple of gunnies cut loose at me. This man here"—he nodded his head toward Frank—"was comin' out of the stable. He sided in with me and we drove 'em off."

The captain's hot eyes shifted to Frank. "Who are you?"

Frank told him his name and, remembering the advice of the redhead, said no more. The captain grunted and went over to the downed horse. It was dead and was wearing a worn saddle whose leather was almost rotted away. The captain bent over and studied the brand. "Circle R," he announced.

Frank glanced obliquely at the redhead, and the redhead shook his head faintly.

The captain wheeled then and came back to the redhead. "I gave you a warnin' last week, didn't I?"

The redhead nodded. "I been rememberin' it. Only I don't

call it gettin' in trouble when you defend yourself against a couple of bushwhackers."

The captain glared at him. "Shibe, the trouble with you is you bring trouble with you. Maybe you better try stayin' away from Reno for a stretch and let us catch our breath."

"That an order?" the redhead drawled.

"Straight from headquarters," the captain said grimly. "We've had enough of you here. Next time you're seen in Reno we'll throw you in the guardhouse and freight you up to trial in Kansas."

He turned on his heel and pushed his way through the crowd of curious men. The loafers, with a last curious glance at Frank and Shibe, drifted away, leaving the lantern on the ground.

Frank turned to Shibe. "I'm much obliged," he said slowly. "Only you know damn well them shots wasn't meant for you."

Shibe grinned and nodded. "I knew they was meant for you. That's why I followed you back."

"You knew someone was plannin' it?"

Shibe shrugged. "Word's already out about your tangle with the Circle R outfit and with Corb. Morg Wheelon did the same thing, and he's dead."

Frank's attention narrowed. "You knew Morg, you say?"

"I was the last man to see him alive." Shibe said. He grinned. "Somebody can't forget that, and they're afraid of what I might know. That's what Captain Arthur meant by me makin' trouble. They've tried three times in the last month to nail me."

"Why'd you tell me to let you talk?"

Shibe grinned again. "The army's the only law we got around here, and they're already down on me, so it don't matter. But I figured it won't be long before you'll be standin' up on your hind legs and talkin' back to some of these ranahans, and the longer you keep away from the army the longer you can stand."

Frank looked sharply at the redhead. It was almost as if his mind had been read. He said, nodding toward the horse, "That's a Circle R brand."

"Don't mean a thing. It was probably stole."

"Know who those men were?"

Shibe shook his head. Frank regarded him thoughtfully, then said, "You ridin' the grub line, Shibe?"

"I would if there was a grub line to ride."

"It's a funny thing," Frank murmured, his eyes baleful. "Ever since I got here I been askin' questions, and I been gettin' no answers. I been standing up, and somebody keeps tryin' to knock me down. All right. I know what I got to know now. Me, I'm gettin' down on all four and askin' no more questions, and I aim to bite somebody. How does it sound to you?"

"Like Morg Wheelon, partner," Shibe drawled.

Frank put out his hand. "We might's well howl together then, because you're workin' for me, Red."

Red Shibe looked at the hand and then glanced up. "I've got a bad name, you know."

"You got nothin' on me," Frank said. "When I get through doin' what I'm goin' to do I'll have one too."

And then Red Shibe gripped his hand, and his smile was wholly friendly.

Chapter III

RIDING BACK TO THE WAGON through the night, Frank listened to what Red Shibe had to say. It was only a variation of what Barnes and Edith Fairing had told him, only with more background and a kind of shrewd understanding. Shibe had done Morg a good turn, and Morg had given him work during the winter putting up the shack. Morg had promised him a riding job, but Red, understanding that a crew was coming up with Frank from Texas, was slow to accept it unless they needed him. That was the agreement then, that he and Morg would talk with Frank. And then Morg was murdered and Circle R moved in, and Red kept his counsel, waiting for Frank.

Every word Red said added to Frank's determination, and he was silent most of the ride. Sometime after midnight they put their horses down the slope toward the wagon. It was dark, and the fire was long since out.

Frank rode up to the camp, but before he was even close someone called out into the night, "Stay where you are!"

"It's me, Frank."

"Oh." It was Beach Freeman's voice. "All right, Frank."

Beach struck a match then, and the fire, already laid, was

lighted, and as it ate its way into the brush and lighted up the camp Frank and Shibe rode into view. The crew was wakening, and Otey Fleer came up out of his blankets.

Frank pulled up and looked around him. The chuck wagon was laying on its side in the rim of the fire's light. Cans of food, flour, grub of all sorts were scattered around in broken boxes. The rank clinging smell of burned wool troubled Frank until he noticed that most of his crew was sleeping on pulled grass and shared one blanket between two of them.

His eyes finally settled on Otey. "What happened?"

"Just a visit from your neighbors," Otey said calmly. He was studying Red Shibe with a hard suspicion. "Who's this?"

"Tell it, man!" Frank said impatiently. "Did the Circle R wreck the camp?"

Otey's suspicious gaze shuttled from Red back to Frank, and he nodded. "That's about it. Ten-fifteen of them rode over this evenin' after dark. They was lookin' for you to make good on your brag, they said. They held guns on us and wrecked the wagon, smashed what they could, scattered the grub, burned our blankets and told us to get the hell off their range before they got mad at us."

Frank's whole crew was watching him. Beach Freeman had been guarding camp, and because he was the youngest the concern in his face was the deepest. The bald cook, Joe Vandermeer, sucked at a piece of grass and watched Frank with cynical and disillusioned eyes. Mitch, Henry and Samse, middle aged and younger than Otey, studied Frank with veiled indifference. Their boss had been shamed, and now a strong crew had warned them off.

Frank, looking at them, came to a sudden decision. He had been crowded as far as he was going to be, and he might just as well start making good his brag to Milabel right now. He dismounted and said curtly, "Samse, go round up the horses." To Otey he said, "Did they get the case of shells?"

"No."

Frank looked at the crew. "I'm goin' to move in that shack like I said I would, and there's goin' to be trouble. Any of you don't like it, now's the time to ride out."

There was a short silence, and then Beach Freeman said, "But we're only six, Frank. Hell, they claim twenty-odd all told, I hear."

"Not six. We've got seven," Frank said. He remembered then that he hadn't introduced Red, and he did so. Nobody shook hands with him or paid any attention to him.

In fact, nobody said anything at all. "Well, speak up," Frank said shortly. "Beach, you want to quit?"

"Not if the others don't," Beach said surlily. "I can take what the rest of you can."

"Then break out that case of shells," Frank said. "We're movin.' "

An hour or so before daylight they pulled out of the camp, fording the stream and heading up the north slope, and the limping chuck wagon followed them with the salvaged grub and the few blankets. And long before false dawn touched the east Red Shibe had scattered them in the live-oak thicket that stretched down to almost touch Morg Wheelon's shack. The chuck wagon was left back in the timber, and the cook was given a rifle. And then silence settled on the coming dawn and they waited.

As it became lighter Frank surveyed the house from his position behind a tree midway between the house and the corrals. The chimney in the cookshack lean-to was already streaming smoke, and the lamp was lighted in the house. Presently, as daylight came, the lamp was doused and there was the sound of voices. Shortly afterward the first rider, after-breakfast cigarette in his mouth, drifted out to the corral. He saddled a horse and rode out into the horse pasture and drove in the remuda, and afterward the riders came out in twos and threes, heading for the corral and the day's work.

When the ninth man left the house and hurried to catch up with the others Frank looked over at Red, who was bellied down behind a thick-trunked live oak. Red nodded.

Frank lifted his rifle, sighted a foot behind the walking puncher's heels and let go. The shot bellowed out to break the morning stillness, raising a slapping echo in the valley.

The puncher wheeled, mouth gaping, looking off into the timber. Beach Freeman, from further toward the corrals, shot then. No geyser of dust marked the spot where the slug hit, but it must have been close, for the puncher turned and streaked for the corrals. Red's gun joined in and then Samse's, hastening his flight. Somebody yelled in the corrals, and four heads poked up over the top of the corral bars and then ducked down again as a fusillade of shots winged over them.

Their answering shots were not long in coming, and, as Frank expected, they were six guns and not rifles. Satisfied, he crawled back into the timber, circled, and when the shack was between himself and the corral he came forward to the edge of the timber close to the lean-to. The cook was nowhere in sight, and the shots beyond pounded steadily and often, keeping the crew driven to the shelter of the barns and the corrals. Frank studied the shack a moment, listening for any shot from it, and he heard none.

He raced across the fifty feet of open space, gun in hand, and flattened himself against the lean-to and listened. Someone was stirring inside, and that would be the cook.

Then he hefted his gun and lunged inside. The kitchen was empty, the breakfast pans cluttering the table. Softly, then, he tiptoed to the door into the bunkhouse and looked inside. Against the back wall was the cook, and he was holding open the back window which hinged at the top, keeping his body out of sight.

Ten feet from the window, so that his body would be invisible to Frank's crew outside, stood Milabel, a rifle to his shoulder. Beyond, out in the timber, Frank could see Red Shibe crawling back from his tree into the deep timber.

Frank whipped up his gun and shot from the hip, and the cook let the window down with a crash just as Milabel's gun exploded.

Milabel and the cook wheeled—to look into the steady barrel of Frank's Colt.

"Drop it," Frank said softly to Milabel.

The surprise on the big foreman's face tightened into a savage anger, and for a moment Frank wondered if he would take the chance of levering in a shell and shooting before he was downed. Then the rifle clattered to the floor, and Milabel slowly raised his big hands over his head.

"You can't get away with it, Christian!" he said. "We'll wipe this place off the map tomorrow."

"You won't," Frank said. "You won't be wipin' anything except your nose." His glance shifted to the cook. "You, go out that door and high-tail it for the corrals."

The cook licked his lips, an expression of stark fear creeping into his slack face. "I'll git shot," he said.

"Here or out there, take your choice," Frank said.

The cook slowly circled the room, his hands above his head, looked desperately at Milabel for a sign that was not given, and then he paused in the doorway. Beyond the corner of the house, he knew, he would be fair game for what seemed to be fifty rifles back in the timber.

Frank shot once at the cook's feet, and with a cry of terror the cook started to run. Frank knew that nobody would shoot him, although they would hurry his flight until he reached the corrals.

Frank took Milabel's guns, threw them out the door, then settled his back against the wall and regarded the foreman, not saying anything. The hammering of the shots from the timber, the answering shots from the corral, beat a steady tattoo in the morning air.

"What are you waitin' for!" Milabel said angrily. "Shoot and get it over with!"

Frank grinned. "It'll come in a minute."

He heard boots pounding in the kitchen, and then Red Shibe appeared in the doorway. Without looking at him Frank tossed his gun over to Red, and it was caught. Frank took off his Stetson, laid it on the table and spoke softly. "You started somethin' I didn't rightly get time to finish the other night, Milabel."

Milabel's hands slowly came down to his sides. "So that's it," he said. "If I lick you, I get a shot in the back."

"If you lick me," Frank said dryly, "I'll shoot myself in the back."

He overturned the table against the wall in one big heave, and there was nothing between him and Milabel except fifteen feet of clear floor space.

"I hate to let you drag back to that board of directors you call a boss with the wrong ideas in your head," Frank said. "I made a brag the other night. I'll make another one. I'll pull those leather ears off your thick head and stuff them up your nose, Milabel. And I'm comin' over now."

Milabel wrenched his hat off his head, sailed it into a corner and lunged across at Frank, one arm cocked below his waist for a sledge-hammer blow. It was nice aim, nice timing, and it would have felled an ox. Only it never landed. Frank stepped inside the swing, let it wrap around his neck, shot a hook into Milabel's soft belly; and when Milabel jackknifed Frank raised a shoulder to catch Milabel's chin. His jaw clacked shut and he was straightened up, and then Frank put a flat palm in the man's face and shoved, and Milabel sat down abruptly. The satisfaction in his face had given way to surprise.

Frank drawled, "Hell, stand up. I haven't hit you yet."

Milabel came to his feet with a growl. Frank stepped back, grinning wolfishly. Milabel had an inch on Frank's even six feet and forty pounds over Frank's one hundred and seventy, and confident that this would tell in the end, he rushed in again, arms flailing. Frank met him, chopping down on Milabel's thick arms, and then his fist drove into Milabel's face like a two-by-four battering-ram. Then both of them forgot what skill they had ever acquired and stood toe to toe, slugging. It was like a fight in some dim jungle, vicious and savage and deadly; and the only sounds were the solid smacking of driven bone on flesh and the grunting gusty breathing.

Frank was aiming for Milabel's face, which the big man did not try to guard, and slowly Frank chopped blow after sickening blow into it, cutting Milabel's lips, flattening his face, tearing an eyebrow until the blood streamed down into his face and blinded him. And then Milabel, dazed and his fury riding every wild swing, was getting sanity pounded into him. He backed up a step, and like a tiger scenting the kill, Frank stepped in, his blows surer, more savage, swifter. He hooked a left into Milabel's midriff, and the big foreman grunted and rocked back on his heels, and Frank lashed out, all his weight behind a blow that struck Milabel on the shelving point of his jaw and skidded alongside it to tear his ear. Milabel's head went back, and he tripped and fell on his back and rolled over. He came to his feet groggily, and now he had a bench in both hands.

Frank said, without looking at Shibe, "Let him go, Red," and Milabel, cursing through swollen lips, threw the bench. It was too big to dodge, and Frank caught it, and the weight of it sent him sprawling. Milabel lunged for him, his tramp shaking the house. Frank rolled and came up, and with one wicked cutting blow he knocked Milabel down. The foreman came unsteadily to his feet, his guard not yet up, and Frank knocked him down again.

Shaking his head, Milabel shoved himself erect, and Frank hit him again in the face and harder. And when Milabel started to slump again Frank caught him by the shirt front and held him and slugged time and again, until the foreman's head rolled on his neck and he was staring unseeing at the floor. Frank caught his weight and said pantingly to Shibe, "Give me a hand, Red."

Red, his face tight and a little strained, came up and Frank said, "Throw him through the door."

"He's had enough, Frank."

Frank's wicked eyes laid their hot glare on Shibe, and he said thickly, "I'm goin' all the way, Red! Get away if you don't like it!"

Red took hold of Milabel's belt, and together they threw him through the door out into the hard-packed dirt of the yard. He lit with a grunt, skidded a few feet and was utterly motionless. Hands on hips, panting, Frank said, "Call the crew off."

Shibe stepped to the back window and called to the men to hold their fire, and the shots dribbled off into silence.

Frank stepped out under the porch and called to the corral, "Come and get your boss man, you riders."

There was a long silence in the corrals, and then the cook, still in shirt sleeves, and another man walked tentatively out of the corral into sight. They kept looking at the timber, but the guns were silent up there. The cook and the puncher tramped across the yard and hauled up beside Milabel, their veiled glances on Frank.

Frank said, "Tote him off the place. Drive your horses off too, and if a Circle R rider shows his face on this lease again, he'll know what kind of a welcome we'll give him."

The rider, a wedge-faced and dirty Texan, said shortly, "We'll be back."

He and the cook stooped and caught Milabel under the arms, and because of the big man's weight they dragged him across to the corral, trailing twin furrows in the dust where his boots dug in.

Slowly, then, Frank's crew drifted up to the house, watching the Circle R riders saddle up, gather their remuda and turn it out. Last of all came a team and buckboard driven by the cook, and Milabel's limp body was slacked on its bed. They filed off toward the west, the Circle R men silent and furious under the slacked rifles of Frank's crew.

When they were out of sight Red Shibe stirred faintly and looked at Frank and then at Otey. Otey shook his head soberly, regarding Frank.

"All right," Frank said. "Bring the wagon in, Joe, and unload. We're home."

Chapter IV

By NEXT MORNING the Circle R had not retaliated, and Frank, taking Samse with him to round up the remainder of the horses, had left orders for Red and Otey to stay at the house and for the others to scatter into the timber and up and down the creek to keep watch.

Otey, still suspicious of Red Shibe, had drifted out to the wagonshed after breakfast and was contemplating the black-smithing job necessary on the wagon. His examination was superficial, however, for Otey was thinking of other things. Ten men had left this place yesterday, ten mad men, and they would join another twenty men who would be just as angry when they heard the story of the eviction.

Otey looked uneasily down toward the creek and shook his head and tried to put it out of his mind. He was a little sad, for he had seen what could happen to stubborn men, rash men, and he liked Frank. He brought his attention to bear on the wagon, squatting down to see if the timbers of the frame were sprung. From underneath it he saw, standing in the doorway, a man's boots, and he raised up to find Red Shibe looking at him.

They stared at each other a long moment, Otey's seamed face resentful and suspicious.

Red said, "Old-timer, it's about time you and me made medicine."

"How come that?" Otey said distantly.

"I'm here to stay," Red said "I like the boss. So do you, unless I'm wrong."

"I like him," Otey said. "I don't much like the company he picks up."

Red squatted against the doorway and said sparely, "Me too," and looked squarely at Otey.

Dislike stirred in Otey's eyes, and he said dryly, "But I ain't quittin', mister."

"Neither am I," Red said, leaving the argument at dead-lock.

Otey spat and came around the wagon to face Red. "I'm an old man," Otey said grimly. "I know cattle, and I can run 'em.

27

I also know people, and by God I can run them too. Nobody likes the kind of man Frank is goin' to turn into. And I reckon you had somethin' to do with turnin' him into it."

"No," Red said.

"He come back from town with sand in his craw," Otey insisted. "He had some before he went. Not all of it."

"You want him to run?" Red countered.

"Other outfits live at peace on this range. We kin too."

"By payin' Scott Corb lease money," Red said. "That suit you?"

"Sure it does. Hell, we're runnin' cattle, not a day-and-night brawl."

"Where's the money comin' from to pay Corb?"

"Sell part of the herd. We'll make it up in two years," Otey said sparely, his voice rising a little. "What the hell's the difference where lease money goes, long's we're let alone to run cattle? More than that, what the hell's it to you?"

"I work for Frank."

"So have a lot of saddle bums, but he's always told them! They ain't told him!"

Red Shibe's face flushed a deep red, and his freckles stood out blackly. He came to his feet, drawling. "The trouble with you runts is you never grow up to the size of your mouth."

Otey said, "The trouble with you redheads is you all think you got to look for fights, just on account of the color of your hair."

They glared at each other a long moment, and Red finally growled, "I don't know whether to step on you or just put you in my hip pocket and forget you."

"Let's see you try to do either one," Otey said truculently.

The quarrel was interrupted by the sound of a horse approaching. It was Beach Freeman. He pulled up in front of the wagon shed and said, "Somebody's comin'."

Red didn't say anything, although Beach spoke to him. Otey was foreman, and this was his business.

"Just one?" Otey asked.

"Yeah. He's in the Circle R buckboard. Gent in a nice shiny black suit, and he come from the west."

Otey said, "All right. Git back to your post."

Red Shibe started for the house and Otey, minding Frank's advice, followed him. They were sitting ten feet apart on the porch, not speaking, when the buckboard rounded the corner of the building and pulled up in front of the steps. Beach Freeman had named the suit, all right, Otey thought. The man wearing it wasn't a working cowman, as his pale face testified. He had a gray close-clipped mustache that went well with his steel-trap jaws and pale cold eyes. He pulled up, looked briefly at Otey and Red and said, "Where's Christian?"

"Ridin'," Otey said.

"When'll he be back?"

"Soon."

"I'll wait," the man said. He got out of the buckboard, only not on the porch side. Once he was on the ground he lighted a cigar, shoved his hands in his pockets and strolled down toward the creek, ignoring Red and Otey. Red grinned secretly, for he knew about Abe Puckett, the Reservation Cattle Company's general manager. He settled back against the wall and rolled a thin cigarette and lighted it, waiting to see the fun.

Within twenty minutes Samse and Frank crossed the creek, driving a dozen horses before them. Red went out to the corral, opened the gate, and the horses, skillfully hazed by Samse and Frank, thundered through the gate and the corral and out into the horse pasture.

Red, closing the gate, saw Frank looking at the buckboard, and he said, "Gent wants to see you."

Frank dismounted and turned his horse into the corral and afterward said to Red, "Come along."

Frank's jaw was set at a stubborn angle this morning. He had an angry-colored bruise on the angle of his jaw under his ear that was swollen, and his knuckles under his gloves were so raw they hurt at every movement. The beard stubble on his face, combined with that look of suppressed wildness in his gray eyes, and his worn levis and scuffed half boots made him look just a little tougher than any man in his crew.

Puckett had come back up the slope now, and he and Frank and Red, with Otey watching, met by the buckboard. Puckett said briskly, "Christian? I'm Puckett, General Manager of the Reservation Cattle Company."

Frank barely nodded, waiting.

"I understand you had some sort of ruckus here yesterday with my men."

"That wasn't a ruckus," Frank drawled. "That was what the army calls a retreat."

The corners of Puckett's mouth lifted imperceptibly. "Well, you've got the place now. Do you think you can hold it against my crew?"

"Why not?"

"What's to prevent them from doing exactly what you did?"

"My crew isn't sleepin' in the shack, Puckett. We're out in timber, and it's goin' to take some work to surprise us."

"And your cattle. I suppose they're safe too?"

"Safe enough," Frank drawled. "They're scattered so far you'll have to hold a roundup to collect 'em, and I can stop that."

Puckett looked down at his cigar and then raised his chill blue eyes to regard Frank. "That may be true. But you can't raise cattle and still fight us, can you?"

"Tell me why I can't," Frank said stubbornly.

Puckett made a gesture of annoyance. "You're a hard man to talk to, Christian. You won't even concede me a point to bargain with." He smiled faintly. "I know I've got one, though." He paused. "I want to buy you out. Now wait! Let me talk. You know our position. We were about to lease this piece of range to join our east range when Morg Wheelon got in ahead of us. We need this strip. Otherwise our crew is split and scattered, and it makes it too easy for others to annoy us. I'm being fair and putting my cards on the table. And I've got a good offer to make you."

"Go ahead."

"I'll pay you cash for this range, if that's what you want. I suspect you don't give a damn about the money part, though. So here's the proposition. We'll lease a range for you from the Indians, title as good as any title here, exactly as big as this and build a shack exactly like this anywhere on the Cheyenne-Arapaho reservation."

Otey had drifted up now, and he said immediately, "Take him up, Frank, and do it damn quick!"

Frank didn't even look at Otey. He said, "No," flatly.

Puckett frowned. "Why not? That's a fair offer."

Frank nodded. "It's fair, and if I was sure you didn't kill Morg and if you'd made me the offer when I come in here, I'd have taken you up."

"Then why not take us up now?"

Frank's eyes glinted. "I'll tell you why, Puckett. I don't like the way you do things. I don't like your crew. I don't like your foreman. I don't like your damn bullyin' ways. I don't like the way Morg died. You may make big tracks, but damned if that scares me. I wouldn't move off this piece now for all the rest of the reservation, not for a half-million dollars. Maybe I can't whip you, but I'm goin' to make you almighty sorry you ever swallowed me! And I'm goin' to find out who killed Morg!"

Puckett threw his cigar away with a savage gesture, the only clue to his anger. "All right, if you want war, you'll get it!"

"I got it," Frank said grimly.

Puckett strode to the buckboard, stepped up and picked up his reins. Then he turned to Frank. "Christian, you're up against Corb on one side and us on the other. Just remember how a millstone works. Good day."

He slapped the reins down and the team pulled away. Otey watched him go and then looked balefully at Frank. "Now you done it," his voice bitter with disgust.

Frank's hot gaze whipped around to him. "Otey, any time you don't like it I'll pay you off."

Otey said, "You want me to go, Frank?"

"That's not it," Frank said. "It's whether you want to go."

Otey studied him with small baleful eyes and then sighed. "I'll stay. I dunno why. I guess someone in this crew has got to have some sense, and it might's well be me."

His glance shifted to Red and it increased in venom, and then he went into the house. Red Shibe drifted over to the corral and Frank followed him. Halfway there he looked down toward the creek and saw a horse and rider coming up the slope from the creek.

He hauled up, immediately wary. How come Joe Vandermeer had let a man past? And then, as the horse approached, he saw it wasn't a man at all. It was Luvie Barnes, and she was wearing a man's outfit of worn levis, checked cotton shirt open at the neck and a flat-brimmed black Stetson.

She pulled up at the corral, and Frank touched his hat. "Mornin.' Won't you light?"

Luvie gave him a civil greeting and said. "Thanks. I'd like a drink."

They walked up to the house, neither saying much except that it was hot for this early in the year, and Luvie sat down in the shade of the porch while Frank brought her a dipper of water.

Finished, Luvie thanked him, and Frank set the dipper on the porch.

Luvie said, "I guess I came at the wrong time, didn't I?"

"Why?"

"You're mad about something. I can see it in your eyes. Still, you were mad about something yesterday. Are you always that way?"

Frank smiled faintly. "Since I pulled in here I reckon I have been. I had to kick a bunch of squatters off my place, and this mornin' their boss rode around to threaten me."

"Puckett?"

"That's right."

Luvie regarded him steadily, then shrugged, and it was more eloquent reproof than words would have been. "Maybe I'd better get my business over, so you can be angry at everything at the same time."

Frank just looked at her, not speaking.

"Dad isn't an Indian giver usually, but he was yesterday. He can't deliver your corn."

"That's all right," Frank said, but he didn't manage to keep the disappointment out of his voice.

"It isn't all right," Luvie said defensively, "but let me explain."

"You don't have to."

"But I want to!" Luvie said. "You remember when we stopped you at the river day before yesterday?"

Frank nodded.

"I guess that was unwise. Somebody saw us."

Frank frowned. "What's that got to do with it?"

"Figure it out for yourself. Yesterday one of Dad's trail herds was stopped about twenty miles south of Reno by a big crowd of Cheyennes. They made a levy on the herd. Thirty beef."

Frank looked puzzled. "They used to shake me down when I was drivin' too, but I paid. I figured it was just grass rent for passin' through the Nations."

"Would you have paid thirty beef?" Luvie countered.

Frank shook his head. "I don't reckon. But I don't see what it means."

"Dad talked to you there at the river. That evening he ordered more corn freighted out to our horse camp. That night one of our men started for this place with the corn. He was turned back by strange riders. And the next day the Cheyennes demanded beef from our trail herd. It's the first time it's ever happened to us. Dad, being a beef contractor for the Indians and the army, has always been allowed to pass his herds through without paying beef." She leaned back. "Now do you see? It was a warning, a pretty plain one."

"Corb?" Frank asked.

Luvie nodded.

Frank was about to say something, and then he checked himself. He stood up. "Well, that's that. You'll stay and eat, won't you?"

Luvie said quietly, "You think Dad's a coward, don't you, Frank?"

"I never said so."

"But you look like you did," Luvie said resentfully. "It's easy for a stranger, an ignorant stranger, to condemn us. But we've got our own way of living."

"Sure you have," Frank said, not wanting to argue.

"Then don't look that way!" Luvie said.

Frank stared at her. "What way?"

"The way you looked when I talked to you in the feed office yesterday! The way you looked at me when you talked to Dad! The way you're looking now! I don't like being sneered at!"

"I didn't sneer," Frank said. "But maybe you're lookin' for sneers because way inside you might think you deserve 'em."

Luvie came to her feet, eyes flashing. "For what?"

Frank shrugged. "I dunno. You're the one that thinks I'm sneering."

"You are," Luvie said. "You think Dad's a coward, don't you?"

An anger which had never been far from the surface these last few days again bobbed up, and Frank said just as recklessly. "Now you pin me down, I'll tell you. I wouldn't call him a coward. He just likes to take things lyin' down. I don't."

"You're a grateful person," Luvie said scornfully.

"Grateful for what?" Frank said. "A promise? Thanks, and thanks again, if that's what you want. It was a nice promise, that load of corn. I almost believed it!"

Luvie's hands were fisted at her sides. She took a deep breath and exhaled it. "I hope you do get run off here, Frank Christian! And you will! My dad has a good business and he's at peace with everyone. But in a foolish moment he went against his better judgment and——"

"Your better judgment, wasn't it?"

Luvie stamped her foot. "Let me finish! He did a foolish thing, and now you think he's a coward because he won't risk his whole business to help you. Well, you'll find nobody likes to help a fool! Most of us here on this reservation can't

talk as fool brave as you can. We don't even try to, because we
know we can't back it up! And neither can you!"

She brushed past Frank, and he watched her walk to her
horse. Her back was as straight as a gun barrel and somehow
conveyed the outrage she felt. She mounted and rode off the
place. Frank looked at the house. Otey was standing in the
doorway, his glance accusing.

So he talked brave but he couldn't back it up, she thought.
In other words, he was a Texas loudmouth, the kind of man
he hated more than any kind alive. Luvie Barnes couldn't
tell the difference between a braggart and a man who meant
what he said.

Frank saw Red in the wagon shed. The chuck wagon was
up on blocks and had two wheels off.

Still smarting under the memory of Luvie's words, Frank
walked over to Red.

"Red, you know where Scott Corb hangs out?"

Red looked up, mild surprise on his face. "Sure. Why?"

"You don't want to pay a call there with me tonight, do
you?"

"Why don't I?"

Frank looked down the slope. Luvie was almost at the
creek.

"Nobody likes to help a fool," Frank murmured, repeating
Luvie's words. "I just wondered."

"Try me."

Chapter V

AFTER SUPPER Frank and Red went out to the corral and in
the fading light saddled their horses. Before they were half
finished Otey drifted out to the corral and watched them.
Presently, when their horses were saddled, Otey said to Red,
"You drift. I want to talk to Frank."

At a nod from Frank, Red went out, and Otey came over to
Frank. "You're out to make trouble, Frank, ain't you?"

Frank said, "I can't tell yet," and stroked his horse's nose.

"That girl was right, Frank. She told you the truth. And it
made you mad. You're listenin' to that redhead, and he's

makin' fight talk. He's got nothin' to lose, and you have. You goin' to do it?"

"You want to quit, Otey?"

"Not me," Otey said. "I give you your first pony, and you aren't chasin' me out. I'll just stick around until they carry you home in a basket, and then you'll have some sense." He grunted and turned away. "Providin' that redhead don't get you killed off first."

Frank didn't say anything. He rode out and joined Red, and he was thinking of Otey. Discounting a natural jealousy between Otey and Red, Otey's words still made sense. Luvie Barnes's nagging had made him see red, and Red Shibe was just reckless enough to join in with him in anything he wanted to do.

Red, sensing what Otey must have said, murmured, "Maybe we better go back, Frank."

"Hell with it," Frank said flatly, stubbornly. "Go back if you want, or come along with me. I got a bellyful of bein' pushed around."

Red gave the general direction of Corb's place, and during the three-hour ride he explained Corb's layout. Corb had come into the Nations to run cattle. He had traded with the Indians before that and had been in the Nations long enough to build himself a frame house and acquire a reputation for easy bachelor living. But long since Corb had given up the idea of running cattle for money. His whisky peddling was more lucrative. He had a slick method of selling it, caching it in a dozen secret and remote places where it could not be found. He never sold the whisky himself; his men were the agents. The army and the agency both knew Corb peddled it, but proof was impossible to get. Any Indian, drunk or sober, who hinted at the source of his liquor was found beaten up, his tepee burned and his possessions taken. Corb had a way with Indians, especially the malcontents, and his position was so strong with them that the army could not move against him without provoking rebellion. Corb was the power in the Nations, and gradually he had drifted into the lease business, the most important of all. Only the Reservation Cattle Company, with its thirty riders, was powerful enough to defy him. All the rest paid tribute to Corb.

Frank listened, and he was sobered by what he heard. He was afraid to tell Red now what he had planned for tonight, for fear Red would try to stop him. And right now Frank didn't want to be stopped.

Frank asked one question. "Does Corb run a lot of horses, Red?"

"That's right," Red said and looked over toward Frank. But Frank said no more. They rode north until Red picked up a certain creek, and then they turned west. Presently a pin point of light showed ahead, and Red said, "We better go careful now."

They stopped under the black shade of two cottonwoods some seventy yards from the house, and Frank studied the layout in silence. The house was a two-story affair with a light in only the ground-floor corner room. Beyond the house the dark shape of a barn and sheds bulked large and black against the lighter horizon, for there were no trees close to the house. A man came to the door, a dipper in his hand, spat out a mouthful of water into the night and called over his shoulder, "Don't you believe the damn liar, Scott," and laughed and disappeared from sight. There was utter silence then.

Frank stirred and said, "Bring your rope, Red," and started for the house, Red behind him. Ten yards from it Frank paused again. The ground-floor windows were uncurtained, and through them they could see a segment of a table and two men, both with cards in their hands. Corb was one, and he had his face to the hallway door.

Frank moved on ahead and stepped noiselessly through the open doorway into the bare hallway. A rectangle of naked plaster was lighted by the glare of the unshaded lamp in the next room, and now the talk was audible. It was careless, murmurous talk of idle card playing and it droned on uninterrupted.

Frank slipped his Colt .45 out his waistband and, once it was leveled, stepped into the room doorway, squinting against the sudden glare of light. He said nothing, waiting, noting another door in the side wall and the two windows.

The talk ribboned on above the muffled slap of cards being dealt. It was fifteen seconds before Corb reached into a pocket of his unbuttoned vest for a match and lighted his short stub of cigar. The cigar was so short that he tilted his head back, and then he saw Frank.

His match, almost touching the cigar, remained motionless, and his black baleful eyes studied Frank curiously, and they were unafraid. The talk welled up around him, and still Corb held the match.

When it burned him he dropped it on the table, and it still flamed. The player next to Corb slapped it out and looked up at Corb and then swiveled his head to see Frank. The others saw him, one by one, and each turned to look at the doorway, and the talking from these five men died.

"Keep your hands on the table," Frank said gently. "All right, Red. Take their guns."

Corb's wicked little eyes marked Red as he stepped past Frank. Then he looked at Frank until Red had taken every gun and methodically thrown it through the window into the yard outside.

Corb said then, in a curious impatient voice, "I don't get it."

"I'm after my corn, Corb."

"Corn?"

"I tried in Reno, but I reckon I leased my land from the wrong man," Frank said gently. "Barnes offered me some, but he changed his mind. So I thought I'd borrow from a neighbor. You run horses. You have some."

Corb's riders quit looking at Frank and turned to regard Corb. He said to Frank, "Take it."

"I aim to," Frank murmured. "But I'm no hand at freightin'. Neither is Shibe."

Corb's attention narrowed. "Rob," he said, "go harness a team and take the spring wagon."

One of Corb's riders shoved his chair back and was rising. Frank said sharply, "Sit down!" and the man sank down in his chair.

Frank went on, watching Corb. "You peddle the corn in this country, Corb. Maybe you better freight it for us too."

As his words died he heard a door slam somewhere in the rear of the house, and he looked at Red. "Get down," he said, and he backed against the wall to one side of the door. Red squatted on the floor, hidden from the door by the table.

Every man in the room was watching Frank, waiting to see if this was the time to break. Their faces were hard and angry and wickedly calculating.

The footsteps swung into the hall, and the man called Rob shoved his chair back imperceptibly, gathering his feet under him. Frank smiled derisively then and moved his gun to point directly at him, and the man subsided, his lips moving. The steps were coming down the hall now and were almost at the doorway, and now they were at the doorway when Corb yelled, "Watch out, Steve!"

Almost in the same second the man in the hall must have realized by the attitude of the others that there was someone in the room. He lunged for the hall door to the yard, and at the same moment Red dove headfirst through the window. He landed with a great grunt of expelled breath and immediately shot, and now the men at the table all lunged to their feet and were held there by Frank's gun. Almost into the corner now, Frank listened.

He heard the man dodge back into the hall after Red's shot, and then there was a whisper of cloth scraping plaster. Frank, gun still trained on the players, moved swiftly toward the door along the wall.

The rider lunged into the room, already shooting toward Frank's corner before he was fully into the room. Frank raised his gun and lashed out at the man's head and hit him, and that was the signal for the whole room to explode. The rider nearest Frank leaped for him, but Frank stepped in behind the falling rider, the other man's hands ripping his shirt sleeve. Corb lunged for the side door, and Frank flipped a shot toward him that chipped the doorframe by Corb's head. But Corb went on through, and then Frank wheeled back into the hall doorway and pulled his gun close to his belly. He said in a wild voice, over the racket of the room, "Sit down!" and slashed a man full in the face who was coming toward him. The man went back on his heels, lost his balance, crashed into the flimsy table and took it with him to the floor, and Frank shot once into the ceiling.

Then a kind of uneasy silence settled on the room as these men froze at the sound of the shot. And above the noise Frank heard a savage thrashing in the other room that Corb had gone into. In a moment Corb hurtled through the door, tripped on an overturned chair and sat down abruptly against the wall. His mouth ribboned a faint stream of blood.

Red Shibe loomed in the doorway, licking his knuckles, a gun in his other hand. He had anticipated Corb's move and had gone around to the back door.

The sight of him broke their fight. The downed man came up off the floor, cursing, as Frank took his foot off the man's hand that had been tyring to grab the loose gun. Frank shoved him away, picked up the gun and said to Corb, "Stand up, Corb."

Corb's black eyes were burning with hatred as he came slowly to his feet. "I'll run you out of the country, Christian," he said. "I'll burn you out and I'll run you out and then I'll kill you!"

"Step over here," Frank said.

Corb shuffled over to face him. Frank said, "Tie up the rest, Red, all except one."

Red shoved a man over beside Corb, and then he sat all the others in chairs, back to back, and with the two ropes tied them all together in their seats.

Then Frank prodded Corb and the other man into the kitchen and picked up the lantern, and they tramped out to the barn. Red took a lantern and the other man and left for the corral. By the lantern light Corb, his spare movements swift and savage, tugged and heaved at the spring wagon until it was near the cornbin in the barn. And under Frank's gun, as Frank leaned against the stall, Corb loaded sacked corn into the wagon.

Presently the other rider, prodded by Red, brought the team into the barn and it was harnessed to the wagon, and then Red and Frank climbed onto the high-piled sacks in the wagon bed and Corb and his rider climbed into the seat.

"Did you drive off their horses?" Frank asked, and when Red nodded Frank gave the word to start. When they were past the house and beyond rifleshot Red kicked the rider off the seat, and Frank moved down beside Corb while Red ducked off into the night for their horses.

Corb was still breathing hard from his exertion, and he did not speak. Frank said pleasantly, "That's the way I like to see a man work," and still Corb didn't talk.

Presently Red caught up with them, and Frank took his horse, and they sided the wagon through the long night on the trip back to the shack.

It was breaking daylight when they pulled into the shack, and Frank ordered Corb to unload the corn by the corral.

The crew was awake and breakfasted, and they filed out to silently watch Corb's labor. Nobody offered to give a hand. They ringed the wagon, watching Corb's lean spare body sweating away at wrestling the feed sacks. Otey looked once at Frank, and his eyes were somber.

Beach Freeman said presently, "He's done this before. You can tell."

Corb looked balefully at him, memorizing the face, and Red grinned. "You're dead," he said to Beach.

Corb's face flushed under the taunt, but he went on with his unloading, working hard and steadily. When the wagon was empty Frank stepped up and said, "How much is it, Corb?"

Corb's eyes were hot with hatred. He said, "It's a favor. I'll expect one from you someday."

Frank counted out some money and tendered it to Corb, and Corb just looked at him. Frank threw it in the wagon, and Corb regarded him with a level glance.

"Nobody's told you, Christian, but you can't get away with this."

"You told us last night," Red drawled. "We did, didn't we?"

Corb stooped to pick up the reins and stood wearily in the wagon bed. He spat contemptuously over the side and then glanced at Frank again. "You made one mistake tonight, Christian."

"What's that?"

"You should have shot me. Someday you'll be almighty sorry you didn't."

He cut the team viciously across the rumps with the reins' ends, and they jerked the wagon into motion. Beach Freeman leaped out of the way, cursing, and Corb didn't bother to look at him. He turned the wagon in the yard and headed north again, and there was something magnificent about his anger.

Afterward Otey looked at Frank and then at the corn. He touched a sack with his boot toe. "What you want done with this?" he asked.

"Leave it there," Frank said. "Before we can feed a sack of it they'll be back for it, and us too."

Otey regarded him with wry disapproval. "You knew that, Frank. What in hell's got into you?"

"Easy, Otey," Frank warned.

Otey walked off, and the crew scattered, all except Red. He was leaning against the corral fence, rolling a smoke, not looking at Frank. Frank walked over and squatted beside the corral and waited for Red to say something, and Red didn't.

Frank said quietly, "All right, Red. Go ahead and say it."

"All right. If I'd known what you aimed to do, I wouldn't have gone with you."

Frank's lean face colored deeply, and he and Red looked at each other.

"Don't get me wrong," Red said. "I meant I would have been too damn scared to do it."

Frank's face relaxed until it almost smiled. He studied the distant creek, his eyes musing, the anger gone. Presently he said, "That was a fool trick."

"Sure it was," Red agreed.

"He'll burn us out by sunset."

"You knew that," Red said. He wiped a match alight on his levis and drew in a lungful of smoke, and then he said softly, "I know what it does to you, kid. I'm for you, all down the line. Only don't look back. Just stay mad." He walked away toward the house, and Frank was satisfied. In an obscure way this was the reply to Luvie Barnes.

Chapter VI

FRANK HAD MADE HIS RASH MOVE, and now he had to cover up as best he could. The remuda got a feed of corn during the morning, while Otey and Red, not speaking to each other, repaired the wagon and loaded it with the rest of the grub. It was impossible to defend the shack now against an attack from either the Circle R or Corb, as they must certainly do within another twenty-four hours. Seven men, trapped in a burning shack, were useless. But seven men able to move, fluid in their attack, elusive in their defense, could fight a long time, and Frank was long since reconciled to that way.

Frank was leaving the house, an armload of abandoned Circle R rifles in his arms, when he looked across the creek. On the downgrade of the opposite slope a line of riders was heading his way. He paused, puzzled at the similarity of most of the riders, and then he knew that this was a platoon of army cavalry troopers in uniform.

He went out to the wagon and had the rifles stowed away when he heard Red say, "We got company."

They waited by the wagon as the troopers, under a lieutenant, received the order to halt in the yard. With the soldiers was a lone Cheyenne Indian, wearing only a breechclout shirt, and a member of the Indian police, unmistakable in his blue coat with the five-pointed nickel star on the breast of it.

The policeman, a half-breed, dismounted first; and then the lieutenant, who was a pleasant-faced young man in blue uniform with the broad-brimmed black hat of the cavalry, followed.

Frank strolled out toward them, Otey and Red trailing behind.

"Lookin' for feed?" Frank said.

The young lieutenant colored a little. "Are you Frank Christian?" he asked.

Frank nodded and came to a halt some six feet from them.

"Then I'm afraid you're under arrest," the lieutenant said firmly.

Frank frowned, looking over the faces of the bored troopers who had dismounted at an order, and then regarded the lieutenant.

"Arrest?" Frank echoed blankly. "What for?"

"Whisky peddling," the half-breed policeman supplied.

The lieutenant removed his gauntlet gloves, tucked them in his belt and shoved his black hat back off his perspiring forehead, avoiding Frank's eye.

"I haven't got a drop of whisky on the place," Frank said slowly. "How could I peddle it?"

The lieutenant turned to the Cheyenne, who was standing silently by, and beckoned him over.

"Is this the man?" he asked the Indian, indicating Frank.

The Cheyenne nodded and began to speak. The lieutenant looked to the half-breed to translate. Presently the Indian policeman said, "He says that's the man that sold it to him. Yesterday noon, he says. He brought five bottles back to Reno and got drunk on that same whisky."

Frank said quickly, "He's a liar!"

The lieutenant looked troubled and said to the half-breed, "Where did he buy the whisky?"

More Indian talk.

"Off in the timber, he says. He says big cache back there."

The lieutenant looked at Frank. "You heard him. Is that right?"

"I didn't sell him any whisky and there's no cache," Frank said, an edge creeping into his voice.

The lieutenant sighed. "Well, he was sure drunk last night. He shot up a store in Darlington and he had a couple of other bucks drunk with him. We damn near killed them tryin' to get them corralled. Then this Indian told us where he bought it." He paused. "That's a pretty serious offense, you know."

"He's lyin'," Frank said.

"We'll look for the cache, if you don't mind," the lieutenant said firmly. "At least we'll make him prove that part of the story."

The half-breed said something to the Indian, and the Indian nodded and went back to his horse. The lieutenant said, "Better get a horse, Christian."

Frank called for Beach Freeman's horse and mounted, and while half the platoon stayed at the shack the other half fell in behind Frank and the lieutenant. The policeman and the Indian were ahead.

Something was queer here, Frank thought narrowly. If the Cheyenne hadn't been so positive in his identification, a man could think that perhaps one of the Circle R hands had been swelling his thirty-a-month wages by a little whisky peddling on the side. But the Cheyenne seemed to think he had his man. Frank waited, wondering.

They went into the live oaks, turned east, traveled a half mile, still in the timber, and where the ground gave way to a little swale holding a tangle of berry thicket the Indian stopped and pointed.

The lieutenant dismounted and gave orders to the troopers to beat the thicket. The first trooper there discovered that the thicket was dead stuff piled there to cover some freshly turned earth. In lieu of a shovel the troopers used their hands to scoop out the dirt, and presently they lifted out a sack half full of whisky bottles. The lieutenant grunted, and when his men pulled up three more full sacks he turned to Frank.

"Well?"

"Not mine," Frank said. "The Circle R was here until two days ago."

For the last time the lieutenant conversed with the Cheyenne through the interpreter, and then he shook his head soberly and looked at Frank.

"It won't do, Christian. You're the man, and you're under arrest."

Frank shifted his glance to study the Cheyenne, who was watching him with those bland, secretly curious black eyes of his race. Frank pulled his horse around and walked it over beside the Cheyenne's horse. He spoke in Comanche, which was the Indian trade language of the southwest country.

"Who paid you to lie?" he asked.

The Cheyenne started at the sound of the Indian speech. He replied in a sullen voice, using the Comanche speech, "You sold it to me."

With the back of his hand Frank clubbed the Cheyenne full in the mouth. It was a hard blow, quick, giving the Cheyenne no time to dodge. It knocked him sideways in his saddle, and before he could catch his balance he slipped and fell heavily to the ground on his side.

The lieutenant palmed up his gun and pulled his horse over beside Frank's.

"That's enough!" he said sternly. "You'd better come along peaceably."

Frank said, "All right," in a thick and angry voice. Orders were given the troopers to save out two bottles of whisky for evidence and smash the rest, and when that was done they rode back to the shack.

Red came up to Frank, and Otey followed him. The troopers were scattered loosely about the place, making a break impossible even if Frank had planned it. Frank remained mounted.

Red said to him, "Bad news?"

"Somebody's planted some whisky back in the brush, and they're taking me in. Otey, you move camp away from the shack and cache some of the corn and grub. Keep the wagon on the move and stay away from the creek and take a look at the place once a day to see what's going on. Red, take a good look at that Cheyenne."

"I have," Red drawled. "He's picked up a bloody nose since he rode in here."

"Follow us into Reno but keep out of sight," Frank said. "I want you to find out the name of that Indian and what camp he's in and anything else about him you can, understand?"

"You want me to nail up his hide?" Red asked.

"I'll do that when I'm out," Frank said grimly.

"You ain't goin' to get out," Red said in anger. "They'll put up a bail you can't meet and hold you till fall court in Kansas and then freight you up there for trial. I've seen it!"

"I'll get out," Frank said. "All I want is for the crew to keep out of trouble until I'm with you again. Remember, that means you, Red."

He pulled his horse around before Red could answer and rode over to the lieutenant and said, "I'm ready, Lieutenant." The order was given to mount, and Frank and the lieutenant led the cavalcade down the slope, Red and Otey looking on helplessly.

On the silent ride back to Reno Frank considered what had happened. The Cheyenne had been paid to give evidence that Frank was selling whisky to the Indians. Two outfits might have paid him to get Frank out of the way. The Reservation Cattle Company, rather than carry on a feud which was liable to bring the army down on them, might have chosen this easier and more subtle way to defeat him. Or Corb might have done it. It was one of these two.

The Reservation Cattle Company would have had time to do it after Puckett met with Frank's refusal, and Corb would not have had time to do it since last night's brush. On the other hand, Corb had the whisky to plant and the loyalty of an Indian who would lie for him.

Before they reached Reno Frank had given up trying to guess. At the garrison half the platoon was dismissed, and Frank was escorted through the garrison and across the river to Darlington. The arrest, he concluded, was an agency affair carried out by the reservation authorities, with the army serving as an augmented police force. He was sure of it when he was ushered into a building on Darlington's main street which was the headquarters of the Indian police. The agent, a Mr. Coe, was summoned and, acting as a judge, held a hurried preliminary hearing, advised by the judge advocate from the garrison, and Frank was held under five thousand dollars' bond for trial in the next term of court in Kansas.

He was put into a neat, strongly barred cell of steel in the upper story of the building. His jailer clanged the door shut, locked it, hung the lantern on a nail by the corridor window and informed him pleasantly enough that supper was on its way, afterward leaving him alone.

Frank sank to the cot and put his head in his hands. Red was right. Five thousand dollars' bail was out of his reach, and the next term of court was in the fall. They had put him safely away and, for their purposes, just as safely as Morg Wheelon had been put away.

Red Shibe, wise in the ways of this country, did not stir from his position across the street from the police office when he saw the Cheyenne come out of the preliminary hearing, mount his horse and ride off east toward the Cheyenne camp in the twilight. He was an old enough hand to know that the handful of Indians constantly loafing about the stores in Darlington knew his identity and would wrongly interpret his getting his horse and following the Cheyenne out of town. Chances were he would wind up with a broken head and a shot in the back if he was so rash as to try it.

But there were other ways. He drifted across the street to the Murphy Hotel and took a chair in the darkest part of the porch and waited for the after-supper crowd to come out for their evening cigar and talk. He would have preferred the bar at Reno, but he was barred from that.

Presently, after darkness had come, the diners filed out, their talk slow and peaceful after the day's work. They were mostly freighters, a sprinkling of agency employees and an odd traveling man. According to their rather sensible ritual they took chairs on the porch, lighted cigars or pipes and talked over the meager news of the post and agency.

Sooner or later they were bound to come around to the arrest of Frank Christian for whisky peddling. It didn't take them long. A man strolled across the dirt street, greeted the porch sitters and announced that Christian had been held in five-thousand-dollar bail.

"A hell of a note," one freighter growled. "Mebbe he peddles whisky, I dunno. But I know they ain't ever arrested the Big Augur around here that peddles it. They jump the little fella and let the big one off."

"They're afraid of him," someone said cynically. They talked around and around the subject, and someone finally asked the inevitable question: "Who turned him up?"

"A wild young buck by the name of Grey Horse. He's Stone Bull's nevvy, but the chief has kicked him out. He's camped out with that bunch of horse-stealin' black sons up on the Salt Fork."

That was all Red wanted to know, and he slipped unobtrusively out of his chair and crossed the street. On the far boardwalk he paused long enough to watch the stage from Caldwell roll into town. Without a pause in the fast trot of his three teams the driver tossed a mailbag toward the hotel porch and shouted greetings to the men he knew were there but could not see.

Red turned on his heel and started downstreet again, and suddenly, from between two store buildings, a voice said, "Red Shibe?"

It was a woman's voice, and Red paused, and before he could answer the voice went on. "Don't look this way. Can you hear me?"

Red nodded and turned his back to her and looked over the street.

"Get your horse and ride around to the alley back here. I'll meet you."

Red nodded again and moved off downstreet. He was more puzzled than suspicious. He couldn't begin to guess who it was and, after a moment's thought, discounted the possibility that it might be someone sent by Corb. Scott Corb didn't know a woman with that nice a voice.

He got his horse, rode down out of the block, turned and put his horse into the dark alley. There was a rider waiting for him behind the store, and without saying anything they rode the length of the alley and out of the business district.

Finally Red, who could not see the girl, said, "I'd like to know a little more, miss."

"I was out at your place yesterday," the girl said. "I'm Luvie Barnes."

This was the girl who had angered Frank so, Red remembered. He kept silent until they were out of the town itself. A quarter mile beyond it they came to a large two-story log house set back from the road, and behind it was a cluster of sheds and barns and corrals. They tied their horses at a tree in front of the house, and Luvie led the way up the porch steps and into the hall.

Luvie called, "All right, Dad," and led the way through a door that opened off the hall into the parlor.

Barnes, in his shirt sleeves, came out of a big chair, and Luvie said in a not-too-enthusiastic voice, "Here he is, Dad."

Barnes shook hands with Red, and his broad heavy face was troubled. "You're Red Shibe, Frank's rider, aren't you?"

"That's right," Red said.

Barnes said, "Sit down," and Red did, and Luvie came over to sit on the arm of her father's chair.

"Tell me about Frank," Barnes said, hunching forward in his seat.

"Nothin' to tell," Red said, puzzled. "He was framed for whisky peddlin'. He's been arrested and he's in jail under bond until the trial, in the fall."

"Has Frank got any money?" Barnes asked.

"Money? You mean bail money? Not that I know of."

"I have."

Luvie came to her feet, alarm in her face. "Dad! Are you going on Frank Christian's bail?"

"That's it," Barnes said. "He's too good a man to stay locked up in jail."

"Dad, you're crazy!" Luvie said hotly. "I'd never have brought Shibe here if I'd known you were going to do that!"

"Why shouldn't I?"

"Because Corb will find out, and it'll make trouble for you!"

Barnes looked at Red. "You can keep your mouth shut, can't you?"

Red nodded, and Luvie said, "Why, besides, Frank won't take it! Not after what he said to me today! Haven't you any pride, Dad? Can't you remember what he said about you?"

"He was right," Barnes said grimly. "I'm a coward and I'll admit it. I'm too old and too fat to strap on a gun and comb Corb over. But that's no sign I don't like to see somebody do it that can."

Luvie stamped her foot. "Don't you talk that way! You're risking everything we have to help Frank Christian! It's not worth it, Dad! He's not worth it!"

"Luvie!" Barnes said sharply. He hoisted his big bulk to his feet, and his pale eyes were angry. "I may carry a lot of fat, but I haven't got much around my heart! I don't like crooks! I don't like bullies! They run a hell of a lot of this world, girl, too much of it. But when you see a man who has got the guts to fight them and lick them then it's your duty to help him. And I'm helpin' Frank Christian!"

He stalked over to a cabinet, opened it, reached inside and drew out a heavy canvas sack. Crossing the room, he tossed it into Red's lap.

"If Frank trusts you, then I will. That's two hundred and fifty twenty-dollar gold pieces. Get Frank Christian out of jail."

Red looked at the money, scarcely able to believe his eyes, then raised his glance to Barnes.

"What's the catch in this?"

"None," Barnes said brusquely. "Bail him out of jail. Unless I miss my guess, he'll be mad enough to swarm all over somebody. That's all I want."

"And next time you'll be having to get him out of jail for murder!" Luvie said. Barnes ignored her.

Red came to his feet, hefted the sack, said, "Well, thanks," and looked at Luvie. "You've made a wrong guess about Frank, Miss Barnes. I can't prove it. I'll let him do that himself."

Luvie's lip curled in contempt, and Barnes showed Red out. He got his horse and rode back toward town, an excitement pounding through him. He'd let Frank stay in jail tonight and get the sleep he needed, for once he was out of jail there wouldn't be much time for sleep. Red remembered the ugly expression in Frank's eyes as he had bid them good-by out at the spread, and he grinned.

He put up his horse at the livery stable, put the money in

his war bag, tramped across to the hotel and stepped past the porch sitters into the lobby.

There, seated in one of the easy chairs, was Otey. He looked at Red with the old distaste, the old dislike, and then came to his feet as Red walked over to him.

"What's up?" Red asked.

Otey said, "Corb has moved his crew into the place, lock, stock and barrel. They come an hour after Frank left."

"Never burnt it, eh?"

"I tell you they're in it!" Otey said. "Livin' there! Settled there!"

Red shrugged and walked over to the desk and faced the clerk. "I want a corner room on the second floor with two beds in it," he announced.

Otey, from behind him, said sourly, "I ain't stayin'."

"You're stayin'," Red said.

Otey's seamed face got a little more truculent. "I told you I ain't stayin'. Even if I was, I wouldn't sleep in the same room with you."

Red turned and took Otey's elbow and walked him out of hearing distance of the clerk. "See that war bag?" he said grimly. "That's got five thousand in gold in it. Frank's bail. Maybe you better quit actin' so cussed and help me guard it till tomorrow."

Otey's eyes opened wide and he nodded slowly. Red got the room, and he and Otey went up to it. Once the door was locked Red pocketed the key, threw the war bag on his bed and sat down to pull his boots off.

Otey said, "Lemme see that money." Red invited him to look, and when Otey hefted the sack he looked shrewdly at Red. "Steal it?"

Red glared at him. "You go to hell," he said, and on that note they turned their backs to each other and slept.

Chapter VII

FRANK was just finishing an early breakfast when the jailer climbed the stairs again to let Otey and Red into the corridor, afterward leaving them.

The moment the jailer was gone Red said savagely, "All

right, Frank! This runty foreman of yours is a tinhorn thief!"

"You're a liar!" Otey shouted. "You say that again an' I'll gunwhip hell out of you!"

Red's face was dark with fury, and Otey was so mad that he was dancing. Both were out of breath, both furious at each other and a hair's breadth from fighting.

Frank came to his feet and said quickly, "Quit it, you two!"

Red sobered down and so did Otey, and gradually, by quizzing each of them, Frank learned what had happened.

Barnes's bail money was gone!

Red claimed that Otey had stolen the money in the night and either hidden it or thrown it out the window to a confederate. Otey, when his turn came, claimed that Red had picked him up in the hotel lobby only so as to have someone to blame for stealing the money while he himself really took it. When Frank learned how close he had come to being bailed out he felt a sick feeling deep in the pit of his stomach. He sat down on the cot, and Red and Otey, sobered by his expression, looked helplessly at him. Red, because he saw no advantage in hiding it now, told Frank where the money had come from. Frank was too downhearted to wonder at it, and he listened despairingly to the bitter end of Otey's story of Corb taking over the place.

"What you want us to do, Frank?" Otey asked miserably.

"Do?" Red said hotly. "Break him out of jail, you damn fool!"

Frank said quickly, "No. At least we got the cattle on grass, and you can run 'em. You try and break me out of jail and you'll wind up here too."

He came to his feet, a restlessness driving him, and paced back and forth in his cell under the grave regard of Otey and Red.

"You're in here till fall, kid," Red said. "You can't stay."

Frank only glanced bleakly at him and didn't answer. Ever since daylight he had been thinking the same thing. And then to have bail within his reach and suddenly vanish was the last bitter pill to swallow.

"Let it ride," he said gloomily. "Go back to the wagon and give me time to think."

He was interrupted by the jailer again. Edith Fairing came into the corridor, looked curiously at Otey and Red, who stepped aside, and then paused in front of Frank's cell. She was wearing a black dress which was not as black as her hair, but in spite of the mourning color there was a vitality in her sad face that made Red stare at her.

"I'm sorry, Frank. I just heard. You should have taken my advice."

"Looks that way," Frank said wryly. Then he remembered and introduced her to Red and Otey. Afterward Edith took a folded piece of paper from her dress pocket and handed it through the bars to Frank. "I found that under the door this morning, Frank."

Frank opened it and read: "Tell Frank Christian if he gets out on bail he'll get the same medicine Morg Wheelon got." It was unsigned.

Frank handed it over to Red and Otey, who read it in grim silence. When Red looked up at Edith there were small spots of angry color in her pale cheeks.

"I think you were foolish to stay, Frank," she said in a low, passionate voice, "but after getting this note I'm going to help you. It's—it's the same slimy way they got Morg, and it's the same slimy people!" She paused, and the wave of her anger was passed. "My dad left some money, Frank. It isn't much, but it's enough to get you out of jail."

Frank said promptly, "Thanks, but I won't take it, Edith."

"It's yours to take, Frank. And once you're out you can do so much more than you can in jail here! Won't you take it?"

Frank shook his head stubbornly.

Edith shrugged and then smiled a little. "It's the only way I can help, Frank. How are you going to get out?"

"I dunno," Frank said. "But I do know this, Edith. Red and Otey aren't in jail. And they were as much Morg Wheelon's friends as I was." Frank looked at Red. "You go with Edith, Red. Somebody might have been careless enough to leave tracks last night. Look the place over. Do what you can till I'm out of here."

Red said gloomily, "All right." He looked at Frank, trying to see some hopeful sign, but Frank's eyes were troubled. Edith and Otey and Red went out, and Frank settled back on the cot and then lay down, his hands locked behind his head.

Whoever left that note was Morg Wheelon's killer. In its indirect way it was not intended to scare Frank; it was meant to scare Edith and keep her from putting up bail money. The effect on Edith had been exactly the opposite, but he couldn't accept bail from her. He cursed softly and bitterly, turning on his side and staring at the wall. There was one way he could get out of here, and that was to sell his herd. He rolled over on his back, staring at the ceiling, considering this. But he knew he wouldn't do it. That herd was a symbol of his right to be in the Nations. It was his backlog and his fortune, and he would rot in jail rather than sell it. Red and Otey would find some way to raise the money.

And that reminded him of Barnes and of Red and Otey's story. They were each convinced the other stole the bail money. Frank wondered about that, and suddenly he came up on his elbow, staring out the window. Presently he smiled crookedly and lay down again, certain he knew where the money was. He filed that knowledge away in his mind, ready for the time he could use it.

His glance settled on the lantern hanging far out of reach on the corridor wall. His eyes were fixed on it, musing, vacant, and then suddenly his eyes focused. Slowly he came up off the cot, staring at the lantern. Then a slow, grim smile broke over his face. Presently he lay down again and was immediately asleep.

He had to be wakened twice that day for meals. After dark, when the jailer left his night meal, Frank took the big spoon, and as soon as his jailer had gone down the steps he knelt on the floor beside the wooden-framed cot. With the edge of the spoon he contrived to unloosen all the screws that held the cot together. Then he ate his meal and lay back on the cot.

When the half-breed jailer, a greasy-looking amiable man who was part Arapaho Indian, came back for the tray Frank borrowed a handful of matches from him and was bid a pleasant good night. As he passed the lantern the jailer shook it to see if it was full and then, satisfied, turned down the wick and tramped down the stairs.

Frank waited out the long evening, listening for the small sounds belowstairs that would tell him when the jailer went to bed. Along toward midnight he heard them, and then he set to his task.

It was the work of only a few moments to take out the screws in the cot. It collapsed, and Frank pulled out the long brace that formed one side of the frame. It was over six feet long, and after he had pulled it through the canvas slot he took the stick and poked it through the bars toward the lantern.

It barely reached, but by stretching he could touch the wire bale of the lantern. He fished carefully for a moment, got the stick under the bale, and then, by bracing the stick against the wall and prying up, the lantern bale slipped off the nail and slid down the length of the stick into his waiting hand. He lifted it through the bars and listened. No sound downstairs.

Then he took the pitcher of water which the guard had left and poured it in a wide circle on the plank floor. Inside the circle he piled the pieces of the cot frame and then took the lamp, unscrewed the cap to the tank and drenched the pile of kindling with kerosene.

Then he lighted the pile, took the pitcher of water, squatted beside the fire and waited.

The frame of hardwood was dry as tinder, and with the aid of the kerosene it immediately flamed into a hot blaze. The floor underneath began to char, and before the wood was well afire the floor planks started to burn too. When the fire threatened to get out of hand Frank poured water on the planks and waited, his pulse hammering. Slowly the cell block began to fill up with blue smoke, gathering in a dense cloud at the ceiling and then lowering as the fire fed it. Finally it was streaming out the corridor window, and then, because the window was not big enough to take care of it, it began relentlessly lowering toward the floor.

Frank crouched on the floor, watching the fire, his ear cocked for any noise. The floor planks were burning in a wide circle now, sending up plumes of choking blue smoke.

Then he heard the sudden pounding of running feet in the alley outside the window. It faded momentarily and began again on the boardwalk in front. There was a booming knock on the door below, and then someone shouted: "Open up in there! Fire! Fire!"

Cursing soundlessly, Frank rose into the smoke and tested the burning planks, stomping on them. One small section gave way and fell into the room below. Through the hole the pounding came louder, and Frank heard the hurried tramp of the jailer running toward the front door. He tramped savagely on the burning planks, cracking another section. But still the hole was pitifully small, and it was only a matter of minutes before the jailer would be up there. He walked into the flames then, burning his boots, shielding his face against the flames, stamping savagely at the weakened planks. Another big piece gave way and fell clattering to the floor below, and then he heard the jailer and another man on the stairs. One last piece barred the hole in the floor, and Frank, risking anything now, jumped on it with both feet, letting his whole weight come down. The plank gave way with a rending sound, and he half fell through the hole. Looking up through the smoke, he saw the jailer's head heave into sight in the stair well. Then putting his hands on the smoldering planks, Frank squirmed down through the hole.

The jailer saw him, raised his gun and shot, and the slug ricocheted off the cell bar. The jailer shouted something to the man behind him, and then Frank went out of sight. He clung to the hot planks a second, wondering what was below him, and then he let go and fell through the darkness. He landed on the corner of a desk in the office below, overturned it with a crash and then lunged to his feet. There was a thunder of someone coming down the enclosed stair well. Frank reached the landing first, flattened himself against the wall, and when the dark shape of a man hurtled through the opening he struck out blindly and hit a solid blow.

The man caromed into a piece of furniture and crashed to the floor, and over the pounding of his jailer coming down the stairs Frank heard the noise of a gun clattering to the floor and skidding until it was brought up against the wall. Oblivious to anything in his way, Frank fought toward that gun.

He bumped into the downed man coming to his feet, and he kicked out savagely. He heard a grunt, and then the man was out of his way and he was down on his knees, feeling for the gun. When he got it he wheeled just in time to see the outside doorway filling up with townsmen. Frank snapped two shots toward it, and they ducked back into the street. And then a third shot from the stair well boomed out into the room, and Frank knew his jailer was downstairs now.

He got down on hands and knees in the dark room and, making as little noise as possible, crawled toward the back passage. Twice more the jailer fired and, getting no answering shot, he struck a match.

By its flare Frank saw he was almost beside an open doorway. He lunged through it just as the jailer fired and missed, and then Frank slammed the door. The alley door was ahead of him. He ran to it, swung it open and ran out into the alley.

A man rounded the corner of the building on the run, and Frank swore savagely and said in an angry voice, "Quiet! He'll take a shot at us!"

"Where is he?" the man said.

"Still in the buildin'," Frank said. "Keep a watch here. I'm goin' for help."

He walked past the man, rounded the corner and then ran for the street. He was halfway there when three men came pounding around the corner on the run. When they were abreast with Frank he called: "Stay here and watch these side windows! He's still inside!"

The others, glad to hear the voice of authority in all this confusion, stopped obediently and flattened against the wall, and Frank ran onto the street. Everything was turmoil there, but he walked into the milling mass of men who were too timid to enter the building. At the same time he heard a shout from the rear, and he took it up.

"Around in back!" he shouted. "He's made a break!"

He hugged the front of the building in the half darkness as the crowd, stampeded by his voice, streaked for the rear of the building.

Afterward, when they were gone, he took the best horse he could find at the tie rails, mounted and rode out of Darlington headed toward the wagon and Red and Otey.

Chapter VIII

HE HIT THE CREEK almost at the shack and followed the dark bank of willows for several miles. The night was black as pitch, and he could have passed within feet of the wagon without being seen. But it was a chance he had to take. His horse was almost foundered, and he knew that the shrewdest heads in the posse that was sure to form would think of Otey and Red first. He had to beat them here.

Presently, out of the night, came a sharp challenge. "Sing out, you!"

It was Red's voice, and when Frank answered Red woke the camp with a shout.

When the fire was going Frank briefly recounted his escape. Even Otey, who had disapproved of everything so far, seemed to be happy now. Frank sent Samse out for a fresh horse for himself and one for Red, and then the council of war was called around the chuck wagon while Frank hastily transferred some grub into a blanket.

"They'll be here for me inside an hour," Frank said. "Otey, you drive that stolen horse a hell of a ways from here and turn him loose."

"Let 'em find him," Otey said angrily. "They'll get nothin' out of me."

"That's just what I don't want to happen," Frank said. "We've got to have one level head in our bunch that can keep out of this mess. We're goin' to need you, Otey. You've got to stay clear."

"All right. What do you aim to do?"

"Red, did you find out about that Cheyenne?"

Red nodded. "He's camped up on the Cimarron with a bunch of horse-stealin' bucks."

Frank threw the last of the grub into the blanket, rolled it up and came to his feet. His jaw was set, and he hoisted up his levis like a man about to tackle some heavy work.

"I had time to do a little thinkin' in jail," Frank said. "I've figured this out pretty simple. Whoever framed that whisky peddlin' on me wants me outlawed or in jail. The reason they want it is because they want our lease. And that could be only Corb or Milabel. And those same two outfits wanted the lease when Morg got it. One of them killed him. I dunno which one, and there ain't enough of us to beat it out of 'em. But it's one of them, and I aim to start whittlin' both down. Once I get 'em down to our size, then we'll find out who killed Morg."

"How you goin' to do it?" Otey asked skeptically.

"I don't know," Frank admitted. "I'm goin' to start out, though, by findin' out from that Indian who framed this whisky peddlin'. Then I'm goin' to strike. I'm goin' to hit hard and I'm goin' to hurt someone, and by the time I'm finished there'll be a price on my head. You get that, Otey?"

Otey nodded.

Frank went on, talking to him alone. "That's why I've got to have a man who's in the clear, who can't be arrested. You're the man, Otey. The only reason I'm takin' Red with me instead of you is that Red knows the country and you don't."

"He'll steal you blind," Otey said bluntly, glaring at Red.

"None of that!" Frank rapped out. "I don't think either one of you stole that bail money." He looked at the rest of the crew. "You didn't see me tonight, you don't know what they're talkin' about. All you have to do is keep out of trouble, watch Corb and the Circle R so they don't hold a roundup on our beef and wait for me to get word to you. You all got that?"

They nodded. Samse drifted up to the fire with the two saddled horses.

"Beach, take Samse's horse and lead that horse I rode away from camp. The rest of you kick out that fire and get in your blankets and let Otey talk when the posse comes up. I'll see you in a couple days."

It was breaking dawn, twenty-four hours later, when Red and Frank rode through the cottonwoods lining the great sandy bed of the Cimarron and saw the Indian camp. Two oversize tepees were pitched out in the open by the river, Indian fashion, and by the faint light of dawn there was nothing awake, not even a dog, in the Indian camp.

Frank untied his rope and shook it out, and Red did the same. Then Frank said, "You're sure this is the one?"

When Red nodded Frank touched his chestnut with his spurs and set his horse into a gallop. Red was behind and to the side of him.

As they bore down on the two tepees Frank waved Red to the one nearest the river and then started building his loop. As he came abreast the tepee he made his cast, and the rope settled over the cluster of poles that crisscrossed at the point of the skins. He slipped out of the saddle while his horse was running hard, hit the ground lightly, ran a few paces and turned. He was in time to see the rope, dallied to the horn, yank tight, and then the tepee reared up on one edge, half collapsed in mid-air and toppled over and was dragged off by his horse.

And from the pile of skins inside two Cheyenne Indians roused up, wide awake and frightened. They stared into Frank's twin guns.

Fifty feet away the second tepee went, and Red observed three Cheyennes in their blankets on the ground. They were still fast asleep. Red kicked them out of their blankets and prodded them over to join Frank's two, who were standing now, their faces slacked into sullen hostility.

Red joined Frank and looked over the five of them in the chill dawn. The Cheyenne who had turned in evidence against Frank was one of them, but his face was as impassive as the others. "Step out here," Frank said in Comanche to him.

Grey Horse shuffled a step ahead of the others. His hair was braided with rawhide and hung in twin ropes over his shoulders.

Frank said mildly, "Who paid you to lie about that whisky?"

Grey Horse answered with a perfectly expressionless face, "You sell it to me."

Frank looked at Red and then tossed his guns to the ground at Red's feet. He threw his Stetson on top of them. Grey Horse observed all this with an unblinking steady gaze.

"Maybe you didn't hear me," Frank drawled, stepping closer to him. "Who paid you to lie?"

The Indian didn't answer, only looked sullenly at the ground.

Frank hit him then, hit him full in the nose, and Grey Horse sprawled on his back. He came up silently, turned and streaked for where the far tepee had been. Frank took after him. Grey Horse reached the blankets and was fumbling frantically among them when Frank dived on him. The impact sent Grey Horse sprawling out onto the hard-packed ground in front of the tepee that was the lip of the cutbank shore of the Cimarron.

Grey Horse came to his feet then, and he had a knife, and now he faced Frank in a half-crouching attitude, a cunning light in his eyes.

Red sent one warning shot over Grey Horse's head, and the Indian maneuvered to put Frank between him and Red.

Frank called out over his shoulder, "Don't hit him, Red. Let me handle him."

"He'll stick you, dammit!" Red cried.

"Let him alone," Frank said.

He walked spraddle-legged toward Grey Horse. When he was close he made a feint with his right hand, and the Indian slashed out with the knife toward his arm.

Quick as thought Frank's left palm slapped down on the Indian's wrist and his fingers closed on it. He tried to bring the Indian's arm up to bend it behind him and got it only shoulder high, and then Grey Horse grappled with him. For a long moment they were locked in struggle, Grey Horse trying to drive the knife down. It was a contest of brute strength, and Grey Horse put his heart into it .

When Grey Horse was straining until his breath came in great grunting gasps Frank half turned and pulled down on his arm and threw his hip into the Indian's belly. All Grey Horse's weight and strength were bearing forward, and he pivoted over Frank's hip, doing a full somersault in the air. Frank held tightly to his wrist, and he heard Grey Horse grunt and then land flat on his back. The knife dropped to the ground from nerveless fingers, and Frank kicked it over the lip of the cutbank.

Grey Horse tried to spring to his feet. He was half up when Frank clipped him solidly across the jaw with a full swing. Grey Horse went down again, almost balancing on the edge of the cutbank. He scrambled to his feet again, trying to dive to one side. Frank's arcing fist caught him behind the ear and drove him over the cutbank.

Looking over the edge, Frank saw him land on his face in the shallow channel of the Cimarron, ten feet below. Frank leaped. He landed astride the Cheyenne's back and drove him down into the water. Grey Horse fought with a wild fury and managed to turn over, and that was what Frank wanted. Frank stood upright, Grey Horse lying face up between his legs, and put both hands around Grey Horse's throat. Then he forced his head under the moiled water, counted five and yanked him up.

Grey Horse was thrashing helplessly, and when he came above the surface he choked and fought futilely at Frank's hands. Frank let him cough for a moment, then said in Comanche, "Who paid you to lie?"

Grey Horse didn't answer, and Frank rammed his head down again. This time he held it ten seconds, and Grey Horse came up gagging, his face turning a dark color.

"Talk!" Frank said.

Still Grey Horse wouldn't speak, and Frank, raging mad, shoved him under again. He held him there until the peak of his struggle was over and then brought him up. This time the Indian's eyes were glassing over. Frank took both his braids in one hand and held his head and slapped him with the other hand. When Grey Horse's eyes focused Frank grabbed him by the throat again and shook him.

"Talk, damn you," he raged, "or you'll drown this time!"

Grey Horse made a feeble gesture of assent and murmured, "Milabel."

"Where'd he get the whisky?" Frank demanded.

"Steal 'um Corb cache," Grey Horse said in English.

Frank flung him into the water and waded out to the bank and climbed it. Red, his face tense, relaxed when he saw Frank come up. And then Red began to curse in relief. He prodded the Indians over to the cutbank and then kicked them off into the Cimarron. Grey Horse was sitting on the bottom, retching into the stream.

Frank got the horses, coiled the ropes and brought the horses over. He and Red mounted and looked down into the channel where the five wet Cheyennes, their faces livid with hatred, were shivering in the cold dawn, and they rode off into the prairie.

"Who was it?" Red asked.

"Milabel. He raided one of Corb's whisky caches."

Red was silent a moment, and then he murmured gloomily, "I was afraid of that," and looked at Frank. "Dammit," he burst out, "a man can fight that crew of Corb's hard cases! But how can you fight thirty men?"

Frank looked at him, his eyes grave, and a slow smile broke his face. "There's a way," he murmured. "There always is in a three-cornered fight."

Red scowled, watching Frank closely. "You mean sell out to the highest bidder and then throw in with him to lick the other outfit?"

"Wrong," Frank said softly. "Get the other two to fightin', and when they're both down jump 'em."

Red grinned. "Fightin' over what?"

"We can fix that later," Frank said. "What we got to do now is make sure this is goin' to be three cornered and not four cornered."

Red looked puzzled.

"Barnes," Frank said. "He's lost five thousand on me, Red. And he's liable to think he's been seven kinds of a grass-green fool for takin' my side. We got to keep him on our side."

It was well after dark when Frank and Red pulled into the dark shadow of the cottonwood that stood in front of Hopewell Barnes's house. Red led the way to the porch of the house, where he paused, made sure there were no visitors inside, then stepped up on the porch and knocked softly.

Luvie Barnes came to the door. "Oh, it's you," she said, dislike in her voice.

"Us," Red corrected and brushed past her into the hall. Frank followed him, taking off his hat. Luvie Barnes's mouth opened in amazement at sight of Frank, and Frank gently closed the door behind her.

When Luvie found her voice she said, "Don't you know there's a reward out for your capture?"

"I reckoned there would be."

"You certainly don't mind making other people share your risk, do you?" Luvie said, anger creeping into her voice.

"We want to talk to your dad," Red said.

Luvie's angry gaze shifted to Red. "I'm surprised at that. We both supposed you'd be on your way to Texas with Dad's money by now."

Red's face colored but he held his tongue. Luvie didn't bother to ask them into the living room. She paused in the living-room doorway and announced. "Here's your two jail-birds, Dad, come home to roost."

Barnes stepped into the hall and did not offer to shake hands. He seemed inclined to be friendly but was not sure whether he should be, in the face of what had happened two nights ago.

Red said bluntly, "Barnes, that money you gave me was stolen out of my room."

"Where did you hide it?" Luvie asked just as bluntly.

"Luvie!" Barnes said. "Let's hear what he has to say."

"That's all there is to it," Red said. "It's gone. I dunno where. My door was locked when I went to sleep and it was locked when I woke up. Still, the money wasn't there."

Luvie said sweetly, "Maybe you just didn't let your right hand know what your left hand was doing."

Red shifted his feet and didn't say anything, watching Barnes.

Frank spoke then. "It looks pretty queer, Barnes, but that's the way it happened. I've come to make good, if I can. Your bail money would have been held by the government till my trial, sometime in the fall, and then it would have been returned to you. I'll have your five thousand dollars by fall."

"Of course you will," Luvie said dryly. "You'll just tell the government not to look, and then you'll get a job and earn five thousand dollars."

"Confound it!" Barnes burst out. "Let these men talk, Luvie."

Frank drawled, "I think your daughter has something to say to me in the kitchen, Barnes. I'm ready to go, Miss Barnes." He stepped over to Luvie, grasped her arm firmly and, in spite of her efforts to free herself, led her to the end of the hall and then into the kitchen, where he closed the door behind them.

Luvie was really angry now, as angry as she had been that morning out at the spread.

"Miss Barnes," Frank said levelly, "you don't like me. Not any. Tell me why."

"Because you've taken advantage of a bighearted man," Luvie said just as evenly. "You're wild and you're reckless and you're a braggart. You're going down and you're determined to drag Dad down with you. I won't let you do it."

"You mean you're goin' to fight me from now on?"

"All I can," Luvie said.

"I don't think so," Frank countered. He was regarding her with thoughtful gray eyes that seemed to bore clean through her.

"Then you don't know me!" Luvie said defiantly.

"I know something about you," Frank drawled. "Something you wouldn't be proud of if it came to your dad's ears."

Luvie was suddenly sober. "What?"

Frank said, "There were just four people in the world who knew your dad gave Red that money—your dad, Red, Otey and you."

"What does that prove?" Luvie asked, her face intent.

"Red didn't take that money. Otey wouldn't take any money, ever. Your dad gave Red the money, so he would hardly take it back. Now you figure out the rest of it. I already did, while I was in jail."

A shadow of concern touched Luvie's face and then was gone, but not before Frank saw it. She laughed a little shakily. "You mean you think I took the money?"

"I don't think anything," Frank murmured. "But I know one thing. You rawhide Red or me any more, lady, and I'm goin' to take that night clerk out and make him tell who he gave that passkey to. It's just as easy as that. Think it over."

Luvie didn't say anything for a long moment. Then she said without much conviction, "You're bluffing."

"Sure, sure," Frank said quietly. "Only I want your dad to trust me, because he's my friend. And I've had a bellyful of your sharpshootin'. Just remember what I said."

And Luvie walked out of the kitchen like a chastened child.

Chapter IX

WITH BARNES'S ACCEPTANCE of Frank's note for the five thousand dollars that had disappeared and his assurance that he was still on their side Frank felt he was clear to move now.

He and Red had slept on the prairie south of Darlington that night, and at the first light of day they were up and on their way back to the wagon. They crossed the Canadian above Reno and were breaking out of the shore timber when Frank reined in and pointed off across the prairie. A quarter of a mile away were two heavily loaded tarp-covered freight wagons in tandem. Six teams of horses dragged them at a snail's pace across the lush greening grass of the prairie. But what interested Frank was the fact that six outriders escorted the wagons, as if they contained a valuable shipment of gold.

"Know 'em?" Frank asked.

Red nodded. "Circle R freightin' outfit. That's a mountain hitch, but they're usin' tandem so they won't have to run so many guards."

Frank's eyes were musing. "Sure of that?"

"It's the only outfit that freights that way." Suddenly Red looked over at him. "Why?"

"Maybe," Frank said thoughtfully, "this is what we been lookin' for. It won't hurt to make sure."

Red remembered there was a plum thicket several miles on where a man could hide close to the road, and turning back into the timber, they made for it. The thicket turned out to be acres in extent, and some freighter, tired of traveling a mile to cross a barrier some hundred feet wide, had laboriously cleared a road through it. While Red waited with the horses in a swale a quarter of a mile off the road, Frank took up the vigil alone. By midmorning he returned, his clothes torn from the plum briars but a look of restrained excitement on his face.

"It's the Circle R," he confirmed. "We'll just keep 'em in sight this afternoon."

It was a dreary business, for the pace of the freight outfit was slow. Red calculated in late afternoon that they would camp by the Canadian that night. And when they saw the wagon leave the faint wagon trail later, Red nodded. "They're headin' for the upper ford," he announced. "The lower ford has a bed that can turn into quicksand under a heavy load. I reckon they're loaded."

"Tell me more," Frank said.

"More about what?" Red asked, puzzled at Frank's curiosity.

"This upper ford. Where is it? How do they cross it?"

Red shook his head, understanding now, and he grinned. "It won't work, kid. There's only a smidgin of water runnin', and they're more careful crossin' the river than any other time. While they take off the rough lock on the shore, half the crew crosses to the other side and beats the brush for Corb's ambush. They aim to—"

"Rough lock?" Frank asked.

"That's right. They camp up on the bluff, and it's a steep slope to the river, and they have to rough-lock the wagons."

"How do you know all this?" Frank asked.

"I used to pick up five dollars now and then ridin' guard. That is, I did until I threw in with Morg."

Frank settled back into silence, and Red, knowing something was up, kept his counsel. He was hungry, but he forgot it trying to puzzle out what Frank was thinking.

When darkness settled they could see the pin point of the freighter campfire in the distance. Frank rose from where they had been lying in a sheltering dip in the prairie and said, "I'm goin' to have a look."

"You go careful," Red warned. "It's in the open, with no trees around it."

Frank caught his horse and mounted and rode out toward the freight camp. A quarter of a mile away he dismounted and approached on foot. The campfire, he knew, would blind the crew to anyone out of the circle of firelight, but nevertheless he moved cautiously, creeping through the tall grass until he could see the whole layout of the camp. It was a sight he was familiar with. The cook was poking the Dutch oven into the coals. Another hand came out of the darkness up the hill with an armload of driftwood. The freighter was straightening out the harness to be in readiness for the next morning, and the horse wrangler was leading the teams, two at a time, down the slope to drink.

But it was the man working on the wagons who interested Frank. The tandem hitch had been broken and the last wagon hauled up abreast the other. They were on a gentle downslope, their wheels solidly blocked. And one of the crew was making a rough lock of a log, which was thrust through the spokes of the back wheel and lashed solidly to the wagon frame.

Frank took all this in, studying it, then wriggled back into the darkness and made a wide circle upstream to the river. Where the ground fell away he had to move cautiously down the slope.

The ground flattened out at the base of the hill, then ended abruptly at a low cutbank. The river had swung toward this bank and was slowly eating into the hill. But from the noise of the river Frank knew it was traveling over a boulder bed and that this ford had been chosen because of the solid footing. Satisfied, he returned to his horse and rode back to Red after filling his canteen at the river.

They backtracked a mile, found some timber, built their

fire, boiled coffee and ate jerky, then doused the fire and lay smoking in the deep grass.

Then Frank told Red what was in his mind. Red listened judicially, and when Frank finished Red said, "What about the guard?"

"I'll toll him over and slug him. If he won't come, it won't work."

Red only grunted, but Frank knew he agreed.

They waited there in the dark for a couple of hours, then got their horses. Riding toward the camp now, they could see that the fire had died down. They swung over to the right and left their horses upwind, tied to a picket stake, and then they split up.

Red walked off into the night, starting the circle that would bring him to the other side of the camp. And Frank walked straight toward the camp.

As Red crawled through the grass he could see the guard squatting by the small fire, feeding it sticks of driftwood. Around him was the sleeping crew. Afterward the guard moved back into the darkness and sat down against a wheel of the wagon, his rifle across his knees. He smoked and occasionally moved around, but he never left his rifle and he never came into the circle of firelight unless to replenish the blaze.

Red had waited half an hour now and he wondered if Frank had given up, when he heard a sudden commotion among the horses who were in a rope corral on the other side of the far wagon. The guard listened, and when the commotion died he settled back. As soon as he sat down the commotion started again. There was a snorting and a stomping among the horses that the guard correctly guessed was unnatural. He rose, rounded the end of the wagon and approached the corral. Then Red saw a shadowy figure come around the front of the wagon, drop on all fours and crawl under the wagon.

The guard came back, looked uneasily toward the horses, stirred the fire, then returned to his seat against the wheel.

Red held his breath, watching. There was a blur of motion over there, a muffled sound, and then the guard rolled over on his side. Grinning, Red rose and cautiously circled the fire and came in under the wagon. Frank's dim shape loomed between him and the fire. Beyond were the blanketed figures of the sleeping crew.

Without a word Red set to work on what they had planned. He took his knife, cut the ropes that bound that rough lock, then helped Frank to noiselessly drag the log through the spokes and lay it aside. They followed the same procedure with the second wagon.

Then they met under the first wagon, and Frank whispered, "Ready?"

"Let her go," Red murmured. They both went to the front wheels and removed the blocks. The wagon did not move. Then, moving in the dim light, they both put their shoulders to the wheel and pulled on the big spokes. The wagon moved a little, settled, moved again, and then nothing in the world could have stopped it.

Frank and Red ran out of the circle of firelight and dropped to the ground as Frank raised his voice in a long yell.

"Yee-ow-eeeeeee!"

The camp almost exploded awake. And the first thing they saw was the wagon rumbling out of sight down the slope.

"Bart!" a man yelled. "There goes the wagon!"

The riders came to their feet, guns in hand. One man shot into the night on general principle and then he turned and listened. The whole crew had frozen into a listening attitude.

The rumble of the wagon down the steep slope grew louder as it gathered momentum. There was a slack jolting of ungreased wood that mounted to a furious racket, and then it ceased abruptly. For a split second there was no sound at all.

Then a thunderous, deafening crash of breaking and splitting wood filled the night, drowning the splash the wagon had made as it went into the river.

That sound speeded the whole crew into action. Every man there started running down the slope, and cursing filled the night with bedlam.

Frank and Red rose out of the grass, ran for the second wagon and set it in motion. Again there was the slow ominous rumble of the wheels.

Suddenly, from down the shore, a man's wild voice raised shrilly. "Look out! Here comes the other!"

The noise of the wagon drowned out the cursing and the yelling as it made its ponderous way down the dark slope into the night. Then, as before, the noise ceased, and then the crash came. This crash seemed to shake the ground, and it was louder than the first, for it had hurtled down on top of the smashed wagon.

After that there was utter silence.

And then Red's brash voice lifted into the night.

"If you want any more whisky, you'll buy it next time!"

And he and Frank faded out into the anonymity of the night, sure that Red's words would place the blame for tonight directly on Scott Corb.

Milabel's office looked over the yard and the corrals, so that when Bart Hampstead rode into the Circle R and vaulted out of the saddle before the horse stopped Milabel saw him.

He stepped out through the office door into the yard and walked toward Hampstead. They met under the big cottonwood that was huge enough to shade half the big log building that was the Circle R headquarters ranch.

"What's up, Bart?" Milabel demanded. The bruises on his face were a ripe purple now, but the swelling had gone down. The bags under his eyes were a deep green, yet he could see well enough. His right eyebrow held a sticky smear of pine tar under which a deep gash was already healing.

Bart Hampstead hauled up out of breath and said angrily, "We got the two wagons smashed to splinters in the north fork. The corn's swole up, the flour is paste, and all that grub must be damn near to Arkansas."

"What happened?" Milabel demanded harshly.

"That damn Corb's crew snuck into camp and slugged Barney while we was sleepin'. Then they cut the rough locks and started the wagons down the slope. They piled up in the river and smashed to splinters. Cove got run down by one and it broke his arm. I tell you, all hell broke loose. I never seen such a mess. And then the horses stampeded and we was afoot and——"

"Get your breath," Milabel said and waited a moment, glaring at his rider.

"How do you know it was Corb? Did you see him?"

"No, but he yelled down to us, 'If you want any more whisky, next time you better buy it.'"

"That's Corb then," Milabel said bitterly. "He's gettin' pretty big for his pants, now that he's took over Christian's place."

Bart shifted his feet, wanting to speak but waiting for a sign from his boss.

"Well?" Milabel said.

"Part of that there grub we was freightin' was headed for Shafer and that herd of three-year-olds," Bart said. "He'll hit the north fork tonight, and he won't have no grub."

Milabel swore again. "All right, have Reilly hitch up that fast team to the buckboard and go into the post and buy enough grub to last Shafer till Caldwell and take it out to him."

"You want me to take it?"

"No!" Milabel said savagely. "I want you to stay here until that crew of rockin'-chair punchers get back!"

Bart turned away and started walking back to the corral. "Bart," Milabel called. He walked over to him. "You think Shafer's herd is far enough away so Corb won't make a try at it to get even for what I aim to do to him tonight?"

Bart looked at him shrewdly. "Depends on what you aim to do to him. If you run off his horses, that would give Shafer's herd time to get across the north fork. I don't reckon Corb would try to touch it after that."

"That's all I wanted to know," Milabel said in a soft voice. "Let me know when the crew gets here. And be sure that grub reaches Shafer, so he don't have to wait."

He turned and walked back toward the house, his face thoughtful. Once in the office, he sat down in his swivel chair, cocked his booted feet on the desk and stared thoughtfully out at the corrals. He remembered Abe Puckett cursing him out for letting Corb take over Christian's place after the Circle R frame-up had paved the way, and he smiled faintly. Corb had gone a little too far this time. The theft of Christian's place was bad enough, but this was rubbing it in. Corb would regret that.

That afternoon, when he saw the freight crew filing into the place, he picked up his hat and crossed over to the deserted bunkhouse. One by one the weary crew filed in, and when they were all assembled Milabel began to talk. The first twenty minutes he administered a verbal rawhiding that left every man in the crew red faced and cursing. After that he settled down to business and was eventually interrupted by the clanging of the supper gong.

The crew ate in silence, afterward returning to the corrals. Eighteen men saddled up and rode off in pairs toward the east. An old buckboard left the place too, Milabel driving out alone. By dark the Circle R was deserted except for the cook.

The dozen horses stamped impatiently in the night gloom of the live oaks, and all the talk among the men afoot was carried on in whispers. Presently, when two riders approached and dismounted, Milabel's voice, thick and almost indifferent, said, "Well?"

"We cut the fence and drove out every head of horses," one of the riders said.

"Is there a light in the shack?"

"No. There's a guard on the porch, though."

Milabel's cigarette arced out and fell to the ground, making a shower of sparks.

"I'll give you fifteen minutes to find your positions. After that you know what to do."

He and Bart moved off into the timber with six other men. One by one the men dropped away in the darkness. Now Milabel walked softly, for he was on the edge of the clearing toward the house. When he picked up the rank smell of kerosene he went more cautiously. Presently his hand touched the buckboard and he stopped, squatting on his heels and watching the dark bulk of the shack beyond and below the trees. It hadn't been as much of a job as he thought it would be. Six men had carried the light buckboard on their shoulders through the timber, and they had contrived to do it silently enough that the shack hadn't been alarmed.

When he judged the time was up he struck a match, held it under his coat and glanced at his watch. Twenty minutes had passed. Then he looked around at Bart, nodded and threw the match up into the buckboard. There was a soft explosion as the kerosene-soaked rags caught fire. Bart knocked the block out from under the front wheel on his side, Milabel did the same, and then they gave the buckboard a shove.

Some of the full gallon cans of kerosene slopped over, adding to the fire.

The buckboard trundled noisily down the slope, and at the same time the first hammering of shots out by the front porch broke the night.

The buckboard gathered speed, slopping burning kerosene onto the ground. Its tongue had been wired up, its wheel set. It headed straight for the lean-to cookshack.

It just missed the corner of the house and crashed into the lean-to, whose boards gave way. Then the buckboard stopped abruptly, and the filled cans of kerosene slopped forward in a shower of fire.

Bart was already firing at the back window. Milabel drew back into the forest and circled around to the edge of the timber where he could see the front porch.

There were answering shots from the shack. The lean-to was wholly ablaze now, and the flames were eating into the logs of the main shack.

It didn't take long for the first man to make a break. He tried it through the kitchen door, because it was nearest to the timber, and he didn't get ten steps before the fusillade of gunfire felled him and he lay quiet.

The burning shack was lighting up the night now, and by the aid of its light Milabel could pick out the place where each of his men was forted up. He didn't realize he was visible until a Corb slug ripped some bark off the tree against which he was leaning. He dodged behind the tree and calmly watched the fire take its course.

Presently another rider made a break for the corrals and the barn. He almost made it, but he went down too. And now the night was light as day, and Milabel chuckled. When the shooting died down temporarily he raised his great booming voice in the night: "Corb! Oh, Corb!"

Above the crackling of the fire Corb's voice lifted in a wild curse. "Damn your soul, Milabel!"

"Next time you aim to wreck my wagons, think twice about it!"

On the heel of his shout the men in the shack made a break out the burning kitchen for the timber. There were six of them, and among them was Corb.

All the guns of the Circle R crew opened up, but they were caught off guard. One man, the last, went down on the edge of the timber, and the rest vanished into its depths.

Milabel, seeing he would be cut off from his retreat if he didn't hurry, plunged back into the live oaks and ran for his horses.

One by one the Circle R hands drifted back into the timber, got a horse and faded into the night. When Milabel's count was right he too rode off alone, looking back toward the shack when he was clear of the timber.

And lifting over the black line of the timber was a faint glow that crawled to the stars. Satisfied, Milabel didn't look back again.

Chapter X

OTEY'S WAGON had swung far over to the east side of the range, and when Frank and Red spotted it in mid-morning, after wrecking Milabel's freight wagons, they didn't go near it. Instead they offsaddled beside a thicket of cottonwood saplings, threw down their bedrolls in its screening cover and slept. The wagon was too dangerous in daytime.

It was late afternoon when Frank awoke, and quietly, without waking Red, he picked up his blankets and saddle and trudged over the rise of ground and the few hundred yards of prairie to the chuck wagon. Joe Vandermeer, the cook, was the only man there; and he was asleep in the wagon.

At Frank's entrance he rose, and when Frank announced he was hungry enough to eat a folded tarp Joe took pity on him and brought out some cold steak while Frank built a fire for coffee.

"Where's everybody?" Frank asked, yawning.

"Otey and most of the boys are ridin' our east line," Joe told him. "Beach, he's in Reno after grub, like he always is. He's pretty restless, I reckon."

By the time the coffee was boiling Red Shibe strolled in, a broad grin on his face at the sight of food.

When they were halfway through the meal Beach Freeman rode into camp, dumped the sack of grub in the chuck wagon and squatted down opposite Frank and Red. He was a thin-faced kid with that wild touchy look about him that is often bred when a youngster is thrown on his own too early in life. But he was a good hand, and Frank had taken him on in the belief that association with older men and hard work would make him forget the saloons and gambling tables and the wild bunch. Joe Vandermeer's words disturbed him. Beach, through the lack of steady work assigned him each day, was drifting back to the saloon crowd, and there was nothing Frank could do about it until this lease business was settled. He spoke to Beach with more friendliness than usual then.

"Gettin' fed up with this boardin'house on wheels, Beach?"

Beach grinned and poked the fire. "Sort of," he said. There was a strange brightness in his eyes as he brought out a sack of tobacco and rolled a smoke.

"I heard some talk at the sutler's store at the post," Beach announced presently.

"Like what?"

"Like Corb and Milabel are tanglin'," Beach said. "Last night Corb wrecked a couple of Milabel's freight wagons, and right under his nose."

Frank looked at Red and grinned, and Beach saw it.

"What's funny?" Beach said.

"Tell me how you heard it and I'll tell you," Frank said.

Beach was still curious. "A Circle R hand come into the post this afternoon with a buckboard and bought a load of grub. He was in a hell of a hurry and headed northwest with it, but not before he got a fresh team from the wagon yard."

Frank's attention sharpened. "Fresh team? Which way'd he go?"

"Northwest."

"You see him hire the team?"

"Sure. After he told the clerk about the wagons bein' wrecked I drifted out to the stable behind him. I seen him hire the team," Beach said.

"Hear him say any more?"

"Nothin' I understood," Beach said. "He called to the hostler that he'd have one of Walkin' Elk's boys bring the team in."

Frank looked at Red, and Red said, "Walkin' Elk's summer camp is on the north fork."

"Sounds like he might be hurryin' some grub up to a trail crew."

Red nodded, and he and Frank exchanged brief glances.

Beach blurted out, "What's the secret, anyhow?"

"Nothin'," Frank said. "Only we wrecked the Circle R freight wagons, Beach." He told him about it, and Beach's eyes glowed as he listened. He laughed when Frank was finished, and there was a kind of longing in his face. Nothing that had passed between Frank and Red had escaped him, and when the talk shifted to other things he remained silent, watching them.

As dusk settled Frank rose. "We'll have to be driftin', Joe," Frank announced. "Fix up a couple of days' grub for us."

Red rose too and headed out for their horses which were grazing near by.

Beach poked the fire nervously and rolled a cigarette and watched Joe and Frank pick out the grub. Finally Beach rose and came up to Frank.

"Can I talk to you, Frank?"

"Shoot," Frank said.

"Not here," Beach said, looking at Joe Vandermeer. Frank, puzzled, walked over beyond the fire, then turned to face Beach. The kid's face was tense, excited.

"I seen you look at Red when you said that about the trail herd," Beach said quickly. "You aim to raid it, Frank?"

"I dunno," Frank said. "We haven't even talked it over."

"Let me go," Beach said.

Frank had his mouth open to refuse when Beach burst out, "Hell, Frank, I'm growed up. You promised me a ridin' job when you took me on. I done all right on the trail, didn't I?"

"Sure."

"I want work!" Beach said vehemently. "Hell, it ain't no fun listenin' to Otey grouse around every night. You and Red are out raisin' hell, doin' somethin'! All I'm doin' is runnin' errands for Otey over at the post and then settin' around listenin' to him moanin' every night about the bad trouble we're gettin' into."

"This is risky, Beach, and——"

"I want it risky!" Beach cried. "I ain't a old man!"

There was a desperation in Beach's face that was a compound of youth, boredom and envy, and Frank felt a sudden sympathy for him. He had broken too many colts not to know that there were times when a man had to let up on the discipline if he didn't want to spoil the spirit of the animal.

He said gently, "No gunplay goes, Beach. You got to be fast on your feet and no stoppin' to fight."

"Try me," Beach said, excitement in his voice.

Presently Frank said, "All right. Get a horse and some grub."

Beach let out a whoop of joy and ran for the wagon. Red drifted in with the horses, and Frank walked over to him and told him Beach was going along.

"You aim to raid that trail herd with him along?" Red asked.

"What's the matter with that?" Frank demanded.

Red looked away. "Nothin'," he said mildly.

Frank took his reins. There was something the matter with it for Red, he thought; and then the old stubbornness built up inside him, and he didn't care. He was boss of this crew. It was tough enough being outlawed into this strike-and-hide way of fighting without having to argue every step of the way. He was dimly aware that his patience was a pretty thin thing nowadays as he waited for Beach to bring in his horse. Red was whistling faintly, and the incident had apparently already slipped his mind.

It was a long ride that night and a fast one, for Frank didn't want to lay over a day unless he had to. Red, as usual, set the pace, for he knew this big land. It was close to dawn when Red pulled up and said, "Listen."

They quieted, and they could hear the far yapping of dogs.

"That's Walkin' Elk's camp," Red announced. "My guess is that the Circle R will use that old army freight crossing a mile below the camp. They'll be shippin' three-year-olds this time of year, and the crossin' will have to be just as gentle as they can make it, on account of the tallow on them steers."

"Head for it," Frank said. "We'll see."

They rode on for another hour, and the sky to the east was beginning to gray faintly with a false dawn. Frank kept an uneasy eye on the east, and as they pulled out of a dip in the ground he had almost decided that by the time they found the herd it would be too light to work.

Suddenly, ahead of him and over the ridge, he caught the bright flare of a campfire, and he pulled his horse around and grabbed the reins of Beach's pony. Red saw it too, and they moved softly away to the east. There, across the flat prairie, they could plainly see the fire built behind the chuck wagon. Two men were moving around it, the horse wrangler and the cook. Off ahead of them, just barely visible against the prairie, was the dark mass of the herd bedded down for the night. It would only be a matter of seconds before the first steer came to his feet and drifted toward the river, and the herd would be wakened.

Frank spoke swiftly to Beach. "You and Red strike north and stampede them toward the river. Don't talk to anyone, don't shoot, and the first sign of daylight strike straight for the last creek we crossed and wait."

They split up. Frank waited alone. When the first shot came and Red raised the long yell he touched the spurs to his horse and headed for the herd at one side of the wagon, letting his gun off into the air.

He was where he could see the camp and hear the herd. There was a clashing of horns ahead of him as the cattle, panicked out of sleep, reared to their feet and started to push. The trail hands came out of their blankets at once, running for their horses, and off across the herd, from two places, bloomed the orange wink of Red's and Beach's guns.

Then the thunder started as the cattle began to move, bawling in their terror to get away from the nameless dread that had passed among them like a prairie fire sweeping dry grass. Frank swung in behind the herd, letting off his gun and yelling. The space around the wagon was empty now; the cook had climbed up on the drop shelf of the wagon and was now perched on top of the box, out of harm's way. A few frantic cattle ran on the other side of the wagon, and off to the right there was a fusillade of shots.

Then the last steer swept by the chuck wagon, and Frank reined up, the reek of dust strong in his nostrils.

Beach, on the heels of the frantic steers, emptied his gun into the air and then yelled while he reloaded. Off to the right a mounted figure loomed up, and Beach pulled over toward it and yelled above the thunder of the herd, "That you, Red?"

As soon as he did it he knew he had disobeyed Frank's last word. The mounted figure shot at him then, and Beach felt a cold crawling sensation in his spine. It was a night herder he had mistaken for Red.

He leaned down over his horse's neck, and this time he remembered Frank had said no fighting. But this rider had heard him call out to Red, knew him for a stranger and had shot. If that word got back to Milabel, the secret was lost. And on top of that Beach found he had spurred into the herd and that the cattle were crowding his horse over toward the hostile night herder.

Pure panic seized Beach then. He would have to shoot in self-defense, have to stop this man's mouth. He swung up his gun, caught the tall form of the night herder silhouetted against the sky, and with shaking hand he pulled the trigger. The man went out of the saddle as though an invisible hand had brushed him.

In sheer terror, then, Beach fought his horse out of the herd, letting the few cattle drift by. In the dust haze he saw another rider pulled up outside the circle of the firelight. It was Frank.

Then, as the thunder of the herd died a little, he heard Frank's voice lifted: "Cook!"

Beach pulled up, watching. The cook swiveled his head and called, "Who is it?"

Frank said, "Go back and tell Milabel he better buy whisky next time instead of stealin' it."

The cook straightened up, peering into the dark, and Frank rode off into the night. Beach pulled off in the opposite direction. Suddenly he picked the sound of a horse behind him and, palming up his gun, he turned and peered through the coming dawn.

A voice said harshly, "Put it away!"

It was Red. In a moment he pulled alongside Beach and said grimly, "That was nice shootin'. He's dead."

Beach's heart sank. "I—I had to, Red," he stammered. "I got caught in the millin' and I was bein' carried over close to him and he was shootin' at me. "

"Why?"

"Why what?"

"Why was he shootin' at you?"

"He saw me stampedin' the herd," Beach said.

"You're a liar," Red said bluntly. "I heard you call out to me."

After that neither of them spoke. They rode on south in the dawn, and they could hear the distant shots of the trail drivers trying to turn the stampeded herd and get them to milling. At the creek, well away from the river, they dismounted. Red had scarcely had time to build a cigarette before Frank's high shape loomed up out of the gray dawn.

Frank said wearily, "That was a sure-enough, center-fire stampede. Couldn't even have bought one as good."

Red said meagerly, "Beach cut down on a night herder. Killed him."

Frank was dismounted now. He stood utterly still, and then he said quietly, "What?"

Red said, "I took the trouble to make sure."

Frank looked over at Beach, who was standing by the creek. "I thought I told you to run, not fight," he said ominously.

"I couldn't help it!" Beach cried. "He was shootin' at me, Frank! I couldn't let him cut me to doll rags!"

Frank didn't speak for a long moment, then he said in a thick voice, "You damm sheepherder's pup! So you're tryin' to hang me too!"

"I couldn't help it!" Beach cried.

"Get out of here before I cut down on you myself!" Frank raged.

Beach started for his horse. Frank, cursing savagely, swung back into his saddle and crossed the creek and struck out south alone.

Beach paused and watched him, his small eyes wicked. "Nobody's goin' to call me a sheepherder's pup," he said thinly. "He better take that back."

Red said bluntly, "Keep out of his way until he cools off."

Beach turned hot eyes on him. "Why'd you tell on me?"

Red said dryly, "I'm tryin' to learn you somethin', kid. You're old enough to take the medicine you make for yourself. You ain't goin' to run away from a damn thing you ever do, not ever. You better start facin' it right here."

"He'd never have found out if you hadn't told," Beach said angrily.

"I didn't expect you'd have brains enough to see what I meant," Red said, an edge to his voice. "Get on your horse and ride with me. And keep out of Frank's way."

Chapter XI

CORB HUNG AROUND FORT RENO the morning after the fire just long enough to hear the talk. It wasn't hard to pick up. Nobody knew about last night's fire yet, but a half-dozen men in the sutler's bar grinned slyly at him. The bartender, when he called for a beer, served him with the remark, "I hear Milabel's havin' a little trouble with his freightin' outfit."

"Who told you?"

"A Circle R rider was in here yesterday afternoon breathin' plenty of fire against your outfit, Corb."

"That so? Where'd it happen?"

"Above the Comanche ford," the bartender said and grinned. He admired a man who could keep his business to himself and admit nothing, as Corb was doing.

Corb finished his beer and went out to get his horse at the tie rail. So this was what Milabel meant last night at the burning shack when he spoke about wrecking his wagons.

Corb rode out of Reno alone, headed for Comanche ford. He reached it about noon and, finding nothing, headed upstream. Presently, at the bend in the river, he saw the wreckage of the two wagons blocking the main channel. He dismounted at the cold campfire and, with only curiosity to prod him, read the story left by the tracks. They were plain enough, from the wagon tracks that missed the cut in the steep bank into the river to the telltale ends of severed rough-block rope.

Corb hunkered down on his heels and tried to reconstruct the scene. It had been done at night and it had been done stealthily, for there were only a couple of empty shell cases here that spoke of little shooting. The camp hadn't been aroused, or there would have been some fighting. And a big bunch of men would have roused the camp. That meant that there were only two or three at most who had done it. And

they had made it look as if Corb had done it, else why had
Milabel retaliated with the burning of the shack?

Corb pulled at his lower lip, then scratched his ragged roan
mustache, his black eyes veiled and scheming. He had enemies
in this country, but they were pretty well cowed. And then
he thought of Frank Christian, because that was one man
he did not have cowed. Slowly he came to his feet, his mind
shuttling to Red Shibe. Two of them, both wild as hell and
tough as leather. Christian was out of jail, loose, and Corb
was squatting on his place. Who else would have done it?

Thoughtfully, using those two as possibilities, Corb again
reconstructed the scene of the wagon wrecking. It fitted neatly,
and he turned back to his horse.

He mounted and turned toward the burned shack, casting
about in his mind for a motive. Abruptly he pulled up and
gazed off across the prairie, all the tag ends of his questioning
suddenly fitting together like the tumblers of a lock.

Motive? Hell, Christian's motive could be read plain enough
in the ashes of that shack. Too small to fight two big outfits,
Christian's idea was to get them fighting between themselves.

And no sooner had Corb realized it than he changed directions and headed straight for the Circle R. He might get
shot, but that was a chance he had to run if he was to see
and talk to Milabel.

He rode into the Circle R in late afternoon, rode straight
up to the blacksmith shop where a puncher was hammering
away on a shoe.

Corb's voice surprised him. "Where's Milabel?"

The puncher wheeled and saw Corb sitting loosely in the
saddle, his hands folded on the horn. The puncher looked
twice, closely, and then he said, "Ain't you Corb?"

"That's right."

The puncher sized up his chances and then went for his
gun. Corb didn't move, only stared calmly into the barrel of
the rider's unlimbered Colt.

"You'll see Milabel soon enough," the rider said. "Climb
out of that saddle and walk toward the house."

Corb did. When he was under the cottonwood Milabel
stepped out of the office door, a look of amazement on his
bruised face.

Corb said crisply, "I came over to talk to you. If you're wise
you'll listen. Send that puncher away from here."

The two enemies, one a big and bluff man, the other a
slouched, untidy figure who looked as mild as a country store-

keeper, regarded each other levelly, shrewdly. It was one of the few good close looks at each other they had ever had. Milabel's eyes reflected a momentary and grudging admiration, and then, not to be outdone in indifference to danger, he said to the rider, "Drag it."

The puncher walked away, and Corb said, "Where can we talk?"

Milabel gestured to the office. Corb went in first. There was a worn leather chair in front of a sagging sofa which he took. Milabel lowered himself into his swivel chair, eying Corb warily.

"What's the matter?" Milabel demanded suddenly. "Gettin' a bellyful of this fightin'?"

"You nor all your crew couldn't give me a bellyful," Corb murmured. "It's just that I don't like to waste my men."

Milabel's face flushed a little. "Come to buy me off?"

"I come to give you some cold facts," Corb said. "Milabel, why'd you burn me out last night?"

Milabel's eyes narrowed. "You know damn well why I burned you out. I'll burn out your other place the next time you raid one of my wagons."

"But I never raided your wagons," Corb said flatly. "That's what's funny."

Milabel stared shrewdly at him. "Takin water?" he jeered.

"I ain't scared of you," Corb said. "Hell's bells, we've scrapped back and forth for a couple of years now. You ought to know I won't run, Milabel. If I saw a chance to down your outfit for good and all I'd do it this minute. You'd do it to me too. But I reckon we both decided the same thing, decided it a long time ago. We both figured it was too expensive in men and money to war it out."

Milabel nodded. "That's the way I figured it, until you raided them wagons."

"But I didn't raid the wagons," Corb said. "That's what I'm tryin' to tell you. I beat you to Christian's place after you framed him with that whisky peddlin'. It was luck, pure luck, because he'd cleaned up on my boys the night before, and I was after his hide. Your frame-up moved him off, and I saw it empty and moved in before you did." He paused. "Hell, I was wonderin' if I could hold the place against you. Does it look reasonable that I'd get you more on the prod by wreckin' your wagons?"

"No, it don't," Milabel conceded. "Still, you did."

"You're wrong," Corb said bluntly. "I didn't. Somebody

else did. And I'll tell you why, Milabel. They figured you'd be mad enough to fight. You were. You burned my place. They figured I'd be mad then, mad enough to turn around and start a grass fire on your range or have the Indians raid one of your herds."

"They?" Milabel said skeptically. "Who's they?"

"Figure it out for yourself," Corb said. "Just supposin' you and me started fightin'. You'd get half your crew killed off, and the other half would leave. Your cattle would be choused around until they was as gaunt as crows. Your range would be burned and your line camps wrecked. Pretty soon the company would decide that they were losin' more money than they were makin', and they'd just pull stakes, wouldn't they?"

Milabel didn't say anything, and Corb went on. "Take me. If you started fightin' me, the Indians would start fightin' you. Pretty soon the army would decide that I was raisin' a little too much hell in the Nations and they'd kick me out. That right?"

Milabel nodded slowly.

"All right," Corb said. "If we was both moved out of here, who'd profit?"

Milabel scowled, alert now. "Lots of ranchers."

"Which ones?" Corb said. "Just figure the one outfit that's got it in for us both, and you'll have it." He leaned back in his chair and folded his arms.

"That's Frank Christian, I reckon," Milabel said slowly.

Corb only nodded, watching him. There was a sudden pounding on the door, and Milabel bawled, "What is it?"

"Can you step out a minute, Chet?" someone asked.

Milabel went out the door, closing it behind him. Corb tried to listen but he could only catch a murmur of voices. Then Milabel started to curse softly, and there were more questions, more answers. Finally two men, one the puncher who was shoeing his horse and another rider, moved past the window. Corb saw this second rider take the reins of a lathered horse and walk toward the corrals.

In a moment Milabel came into the room and walked to his chair, not even looking at Corb. His face was ugly, and a half-smoked cigarette hung from his lips. He looked keenly at Corb and then sank into the chair. He stared at the floor, looking at Corb now and then, and finally his mind seemed to be made up.

He said to Corb, "A herd of three-year-olds Shafer was

drivin' to Caldwell was stampeded up on the north fork last night. About two hundred of them bogged down in quicksand, and there's still three hundred missin'. The rest each run about twenty pounds of tallow off in the stampede."

Corb only smiled faintly under his roan mustache.

"Three men done it," Milabel went on, watching Corb. "They told the cook that if I wanted whisky again I better buy it." He paused. "That's the same thing they called that night when they wrecked the wagons." At Corb's frown of puzzlement Milabel went on. "We raided a cache of yours for whisky to frame Christian."

"I know," Corb said.

"Then whoever it was wrecked the wagons and stampeded the herd last night wanted it to look like it was you gettin' even with us for stealin' your whisky."

"But my whole crew was in the house when you burned it last night," Corb pointed out.

"I know, I know," Milabel said wearily. He dropped his cigarette and stepped on it. "Well, it looks like you're right."

"Sure I'm right. You need any more proof?"

"What do you want to do?"

"First thing," Corb said, "is for us to quit fightin'. We're just wreckin' each other so Christian can step in."

"What else you think we ought to do?"

Corb stood up. "That's up to you," he said quietly. "If you want to throw in with me to lick this Christian. I'll do it. We'll call a truce long enough to run him out of the country."

Milabel said, "There's one thing I didn't tell you. One of my trail hands was killed last night."

He and Corb looked at each other, and Milabel said, "The first thing we ought to do, then, is to have that reward for Frank Christian raised to two thousand dollars. You and me will put up the fifteen hundred extra. And this time it will be 'dead or alive'."

Corb nodded. "Now you're talkin'."

Milabel rose. "I'll think about the rest of it. I'll ride over in a couple days and let you know. I want to get Puckett's permission, and I'll have to use the army telegraph at Reno."

"There's no hurry," Corb said. "Think it over."

Milabel nodded. "Understand," he said, "I ain't got any love for you, Corb. I'll smash hell out of you someday. This is just a truce, see?"

"I do," Corb said dryly. "Those are my sentiments exactly." And he left the place, unmolested.

Chapter XII

FROM HIS SEAT in the gloom of the Murphy Hotel front porch in Darlington Red Shibe had already picked up enough talk to know that he and Frank had made a mistake in stampeding Milabel's herd. For the night they had elected to stampede the herd was the same night Milabel had chosen to corner all Corb's crew in the shack and burn it down on top of them. Milabel would know Corb couldn't have raided his herd. Once he knew that, he would question the wagon wrecking, and Frank's plan would go up in smoke, Red thought gloomily.

Red decided to sit it out to the bitter end and find out, if possible, who was suspected of stampeding the Circle R herd. He was listening to the talk with only half attention when he saw a woman's figure on the boardwalk across the street. She paused opposite the hotel and stared across at the porch.

Red watched her curiously, until suddenly he came to his senses. This was Edith Fairing, and she was looking for him. The day Frank was in jail and Red took Edith home he had left her with the admonition that if she ever received another warning note to come to the hotel porch every night until she found him.

Red rose, left his chair and crossed the street to Edith.

"Trouble?" he asked, touching his hatbrim as he stepped on the boardwalk.

Edith said, "No," smiling a little, and then added, "I think we'd better walk away from my house until I explain."

Red fell in beside her, watching her out of the corner of his eye. He couldn't see this girl without remembering that she would now be Morg Wheelon's wife if he hadn't left Morg alone that night. She was too young for sorrow, too pretty, and he wished he could drive that haunted look from her eyes.

When they had passed the corner Red said, "Did you get another note?"

"No. Scott Corb is at the house, Red."

Red stopped, staring at her. "Corb? Did he——"

"No, he's very polite. He wants to talk to Frank."

"What about?"

"He won't say. He said he couldn't find Frank, didn't know where to look for him, and that he thought I might be able to get in touch with him."

Red said, "Is he alone?"

"He's alone in the house. But he may have men outside. That's why I suggested we walk away from the house."

"Good girl," Red murmured.

"Do you want to take him to Frank?"

"I dunno," Red said. "I'll hear him talk first. You turn around and go home. I'll drift back and take a look around the house before I knock on the door."

When Edith had gone Red swung into the closest alley and made his way by a devious route to the Fairings' small house. There was something almighty queer about this—unless Corb figured he was licked and wanted to make a deal. But that wasn't like Corb. Red grinned when he thought of Frank laying eyes on Corb. Frank was in a savage temper after the Circle R stampede. Beach had been fired. Frank blamed himself for the useless death of that trail hand, although Red had tried to convince him that the man was a hired gunnie of Milabel's and that Beach Freeman was guilty anyway. And, to boot, the news of their blunder and the sight of Corb wouldn't help Frank's temper.

When he reached Edith Fairing's place Red investigated the alley and the barn. Then he walked the street on both sides of the road and even circled the block to see if any men were hidden out around town. Almost satisfied but still wary, he came back to the Fairing house and knocked on the door.

Edith let him in and took him into the parlor. Corb was standing there, hat in hand, waiting. His bland face didn't change at sight of Red, but his wicked little eyes studied him minutely.

"Better leave the door open," Red said to Edith. "I don't like the smell in here."

"I want to see Christian, Shibe," Corb said, ignoring Red's gibe.

"That's a bushwhack trick that's old even for Indians, Corb," Red jeered.

"I haven't any men here," Corb said. "Look and see, if you want to. I'll give you my gun and we won't be followed."

"Frank will shoot you on sight," Red said.

"No, he won't. He'd better not, because I have some information he wants."

"About what?"

"I'll tell him when I see him."

Red leaned up against the table and regarded Corb with grudging admiration. "For a skunk," Red drawled, "you got more gall than a government mule, Corb. You can't tell Frank anything he wants to know. You can't do him any favor, except drop dead."

"Red!" Edith said in a half-frightening voice. Corb was the power here, and Red was talking to him like any saddle bum.

Red looked over at her and grinned. "You ain't afraid, are you, Edith? Look at him. He's just an old man with weasel eyes and a black heart and a snake's brains." He looked over at Corb, but Corb was regarding him placidly. Corb wasn't being baited tonight.

"Let's talk business," Corb said. "Will you take me to Christian?"

"What's to prevent your hard cases from trailin' us and cuttin' down on Frank when we meet him?"

"It's night, and you can't trail at night," Corb pointed out dryly. Then he said casually, "Can't you get it through your thick head I want to talk to him? You've got a wagon and a crew, haven't you?"

Red didn't answer.

"I know you have because I saw them," Corb went on. "Take me to your crew and then bring Frank in to talk." He sneered. "You ought to feel safe enough that way."

Red's freckled face flushed a little. "You're a pretty cagey hombre, Corb. You know damn well I'll take you to Frank just to prove we ain't scared of you."

"Do it, then."

"I will," Red said grimly. He walked over to Corb, took the gun from his shoulder holster, searched him for other weapons and, finding none, motioned him to the door. Corb went out.

Edith said, "Be careful, Red," and her eyes were worried.

Red grinned reassuringly. "Not me. If I could rawhide that coyote into a fight and lift his scalp I'd try it in a minute."

"No, you wouldn't, Red," Edith said calmly. "You'll be careful."

Red looked strangely at her, and when she smiled faintly he gulped, grinned, mumbled, "I reckon I will," and said good night.

Outside Corb was waiting for him. Red said, "Meet me in front of the hotel," and walked upstreet.

Once he had his horse he said, "We'll go out of town my way, Corb. You just follow."

Red started toward the river, but as soon as he was away from the town's lights he circled and went out the south road. Once there, he made a wide swing west and to the north, occasionally stopping to see if he was being followed. Corb was patient through it all, even when Red ordered him to stay set and made a wide circle over their backtrail. After that Red made for the wagon in a straight line, and they rode for two hours without exchanging a word.

Otey's wagon was pulled up in a swale by a deep, wide feeder creek of the Paymaster, screened from any but the most prying eyes by the willow thickets and the high creek banks.

They were challenged by Joe Vandermeer, but Red was identified, and they dismounted and walked to the dying fire. Red built it up, and the crew came awake.

Otey, from his blankets, said suddenly, "What's that lobo doin' in camp?" eying Corb balefully.

"You just keep a gun on him," Red grunted. "He wants to make medicine with Frank."

Red went out and stepped into the saddle again and rode out west. As soon as he was out of hearing of the camp he turned north, and the night was unbelievably black after the light of the fire. A quarter mile up the creek, after making no attempt to cover the sound of his movements, he whistled twice. Almost behind him and close came the answering whistle. Neither Red nor Frank were taking a chance on being caught in camp.

"Frank?"

Red got only a grunt in reply, and he walked in that direction. Presently he saw Frank's blankets on the ground. He squatted beside them and said, "Corb's in camp. Wants to talk to you."

Frank's voice was not sleepy as he echoed, "Corb?"

"That's right. And listen, kid. Milabel caught Corb and his crew at the shack last night and burned them out. Shot a couple of his men."

Frank didn't speak for a moment, and then he said bitterly, "So our stampede was for nothin', then?"

"Looks like it. Corb's crew couldn't be in two places."

Frank didn't say anything, but Red knew how he felt. This was a long, waiting game at best, and now the little work they had done was for nothing. Frank pulled on his boots,

strapped on his gun belt and rose. They rode double back to
camp, coming in from the south.

As Frank dismounted and walked into the circle of firelight
Corb might have been warned by his looks. Long hours in
the saddle and food snatched when he could eat it had
gaunted Frank into a lean, wolfish-looking rider. His gray
eyes that had once been calm were smoldering and sultry, and
the line of his unshaven jaw was heavy and dogged. Red had
seen men come out of prison looking that way. It was from
too much defeat and too big odds, and only fighting men
looked that way. And Red had learned to drink his whisky
and walk out of a saloon when he saw them. He wondered
if Corb had.

Frank stalked up to the fire, and Corb stood opposite him,
warming his hands. The crew was standing away from the
fire, regarding the meeting with expectant faces.

"I won't offer you anything to eat or drink," Frank said
softly. "We feed the dogs away from the camp."

Corb's face didn't change. "I want to talk to you, Christian,
not eat your food."

"Go ahead and talk."

Corb looked around him. "In private," he said in a low
voice.

"Get the hell out of here, then," Frank said.

"All right, all right," Corb said pacifically. "Don't get so
redheaded."

Frank didn't say anything, and Corb looked down into the
fire, feeling for a way to begin.

He looked up presently and said, "That raid on Milabel's
herd was a mistake. You tried to blame it on my crew, but
Milabel had me and my crew cornered at the shack."

"How do you know I tried to blame it on your crew?"
Frank asked.

Corb smiled, and the ends of his pale ragged mustaches
lifted a quarter inch. "I've talked to Milabel," Corb said. "It
was a nice play, Christian, only you were in too much of a
hurry. We're on to you."

"So you and Milabel are pardin' up," Frank drawled. "How
come?"

"It was you," Corb said bluntly. "I was all ready to tangle
with Milabel over burnin' the shack, but he called somethin'
that night about my wreckin' his wagons that didn't make
sense. I took my time and looked around and guessed the
rest, then went to him."

Frank said thinly, "Did you come here to brag?"

"I'm tellin' you," Corb said, "Milabel and me ain't fightin' each other any more. We're fightin' you."

"I'm scared," Frank said.

"You ain't scared," Corb said evenly. "You're mad. But you ain't so mad you can't see what this means."

"You tell me," Frank said.

Corb said, "Whatever happens to Milabel's cattle, his crew or his range, he's goin' to let me alone, because he'll figure it's you and not me that's doin' it. Do you get that?"

"So far."

"Me and Milabel are workin' together to down you. We're poolin' our information and we're aimin' to nail you. You get that?"

"Sure."

"Suppose I get a tip on your movements, take it to Milabel, and we take both our crews halfway to Kansas to corner you." He paused, his black eyes glittering and intent. "You can take your crew, burn the Circle R, wreck all the gear, drive his horses clean out of the country, scatter his cattle all over three reservations and grass-fire his range. He's got shippin' dates to meet. He won't have time to meet them, he won't have horses for his crew, and when he gets his cattle back they'll have all the tallow run off and no grass to put it back on with. When Puckett takes a look at that setup he'll pull out, because he'll have had to forfeit a quarter million in beef contracts he couldn't meet."

Red saw Frank smile, and he waited for Frank to speak. When Frank did it was in a reasonable tone of voice, with an uncertain something mingled with it. "My crew has done all the work. What do we get?"

"You get a clear title to Morg Wheelon's place with my guarantee behind it that you won't be bothered."

"And you'll take over the Circle R range?"

"That's about it," Corb said, watching Frank.

Frank squatted by the fire and idly poked a stick. He said curiously, "That's a nice proposition, Corb. What makes you think I can handle my end of it?"

"I ain't scared about that," Corb said. "When you busted into my place that night and wrecked it you didn't do any shootin'. You could have, only you didn't. I figured you was scared of the law or the army. But the other night when you picked off one of Corb's hard cases in that stampede I knew you was tough enough. If we work together you got to be tough enough to take care of the skeleton crew Milabel will leave at the Circle R. You can do it."

Frank stopped poking the fire and slowly raised his head to regard Corb. His face was pale and rigid with anger, and his lips were almost white.

"You damn tinhorn Judas. Get out!"

Corb scowled. "You mean you ain't goin' to—"

"I mean I'm goin' to kill you, Corb," Frank said, rising. "I should have done it the other night, but you didn't smell as bad as you do now. The next time you see me you better come smokin'!"

Again Corb's mustaches lifted in a faint smile. "You're goin' to be sorry," he said.

He turned and started to walk away. Otey called, "Your horse is the other way, Corb."

Corb had a handkerchief in his hand and he was mopping his brow. He seemed not to hear Otey and kept on walking out of the firelight, up the creek.

It was Red, standing well away from the fire, who saw it first. He ran straight for the fire, ramming into Frank and sending him sprawling, and kicked the burning sticks out into the night, wiping out the light as suddenly as thought. And immediately afterward rifles opened up from the ridges on either side of the creek and from down and up stream.

Frank, sizing up the trap, yelled to the crew, "Don't a man shoot a shot! Don't give 'em a target!" He crawled ahead in the darkness, for the slugs were searching out the spot where he had fallen. He brushed a man who was lying on the ground and he whispered, "Red?"

"I'm sorry as hell, Frank!" Red moaned. "I should have known it when he suggested comin' to the wagon. He's had it spotted all day and planted his men here tonight, just in case you turned him down."

"I'm glad of it," Frank said grimly. "I know where I stand with that hombre now. Get away in the brush, Red, and hold your fire till they rush us."

He crawled to the wagon, stood up, reached down a rifle and crawled into the creekside brush. The shots were coming from seven different places, but they were aimless. The dark well of the swale was black as soot. Red's swift move to douse the fire after Corb's handkerchief signal had saved them all from being massacred. Corb's planted crew could shoot all night, and it would only be chance if they hit anyone. The smoldering embers of the fire were scattered all over the small flat, but their dying glow was barely visible.

Frank somberly considered the situation. If Corb was set for a showdown he would try to rush the camp after he realized that his advantage was canceled by darkness. In a hand-to-hand battle both sides would lose men. Corb didn't care, and Frank did. He had brought these peaceful hard-working punchers into trouble, and he was not going to see them butchered by Corb's hired hard cases.

The shooting from the ridges and from up and down stream increased. It wouldn't be long before Corb gave the order to rush. Frank knew he had to get outside Corb's slowly encircling crew, but to move in this crackling brush was to draw fire upon himself. He couldn't crawl out and advertise every move, for it would be sure death. He moved his hand out through the brush and touched wet ground. It was the creek bank.

Suddenly he knew he had it, and he took off his shell belt and gun. Slowly, quietly as he could, he pulled himself to the creek and lowered himself into it. The cold water, only a little deeper than the thickness of his body, took his breath away. He would have to leave his rifle, he knew. He reached out for his shell belt, put his head through it, so that some of his shells would be dry, and let the rush of the water move him slowly downstream. He could see nothing ahead of him, but the current carried him on. He was approaching one of the riflemen who was shooting systematically at the camp. Frank drifted almost under the man's gun and then past him, and the man did not know it.

Well downstream Frank crawled out, his teeth chattering. He heard Corb shout, "Close in!" and he knew that whatever he did would have to be done quickly. There was no time to round up the horses and stampede them through the line of encircling men to break it up. There was only one thing he could do.

He moved quietly toward the rifleman closest him, who was levering and firing his rifle as fast as he could. There was no necessity for stealth, and Frank approached him from behind, made out the dark bulk of his figure and slashed out with his gun barrel. The man went down without a murmur, and Frank took his rifle and shell belt. Then he moved on upstream and took up a new position where he could see the gun flashes of every one of Corb's riders.

He began to shoot in earnest then, throwing five rapid shots at the gun flame of a rifleman up the ridge. When he ceased there was a gap in the ring of rifles. He concentrated next on the rifleman down the ridge. On his second shot he heard a long-drawn scream, and the firing suddenly died. Corb's men had heard it too, and there had been no doubt that it came from one of their own crew. Uneasiness seemed to fill the night, and Corb's men resumed their shooting half-heartedly.

Corb's angry voice yelled: "Close in, I tell you!" and still none of the riflemen moved closer. There was one rifleman left on the west ridge, and he was a long time making up his mind to continue firing. When he did he had moved, for he could understand plainly enough what had happened to the other two men stationed on the same ridge.

Frank was ready for him too. He laid a withering fire on the man, and the rifle was silenced. Now the shooting ceased. Every one of Corb's men had seen the three rifles on the west ridge disappear, and they had an idea what had happened. There had been no shooting from Frank's crew; therefore, either there was someone roaming the darkness who was silencing these men, or else there was a traitor among themselves who had killed his own companions under the cover of general firing.

Corb's voice came again, and it was wild with rage. "Rush them, damn you! There's only five of them!"

Nobody moved closer to the camp, and there was no shooting. Up the creek Corb's raging voice could be heard cursing out one of his men.

And then someone struck a match in the middle of the camp. It caught, and brush started to burn, and suddenly the whole camp was lighted up. Frank held his breath. Had one of Corb's men succeeded in getting some brush together and lighting it to provide light for the killing? The riflemen started shooting again then, but Frank could see nothing to shoot at except the wagon.

And then suddenly, from behind him downstream and from behind the east ridge, a savage firing broke out. And Frank had it then.

Red and the crew had crawled out the gap on the west ridge, leaving one man to light the fire. And now his crew had Corb's killers between themselves and the fire.

A shot ripped the brush behind him, and Frank knew

that somebody, Red maybe, had him spotted. As soon as Corb's crew saw what had happened there was a crashing of brush up the creek. A man streaked over the ridge and dived into the willows, thrashed around in the water heading up-creek. There was a savage fire out in the night. One man who had been across the stream raced through camp. There was a shot from the ridge; he tripped, sprawled and was brought up against the wheel of the chuck wagon and lay still.

The tables were reversed now, and Frank rose out of the brush and yelled: "Drive 'em up the creek, Red!"

Swiftly Frank's crew beat up the creek, firing ahead of them. But off on the prairie they heard the thunder of running horses, and Frank knew that Corb had escaped with what remained of his crew.

One by one the crew drifted back to the fire. Joe Vandermeer had been shot through the arm, and his sleeve was soaked with blood. His teeth chattering, Frank bandaged him. Joe grinned up at him, and Frank smiled back, but that grin did something to Frank. It made up his mind for him.

Red drifted back, declaring that he had found four of Corb's crew, all dead, and that Samse had better get the wagon hitched to move before Corb brought back reinforcements. Samse turned away to get the horses when Frank rose and called, "Wait a minute, Samse."

Samse came back to the fire. The others—Mitch, Otey, Red and Joe—looked at him, come alert by the tone of his voice.

Frank said quietly, "I've been a damn fool for long enough. I ain't goin' to get that lease back for a long time, boys, and when I do it's goin' to be with a fightin' crew. You ain't gunmen and I ain't payin' you gunmen's wages, so I don't aim to hold you any more." He looked at all of them. "Ride out of here for good and you're welcome to horses and grub, and you can pick up your pay at the Stockman's Bank in Fort Worth. There's no strings hangin' on that offer, and you better take it."

Samse pulled back his shoulders and looked squarely at Frank. "I've done what I could, Frank, and it ain't much. I hate to do this, but I'm goin' to take up your offer."

Otey said quietly, "I'll stay."

Red said, "Me too."

Joe Vandermeer and Mitch didn't say anything, only looked at Samse and nodded. While Joe and Mitch packed the grub

Samse brought in the saddle horses. They shook hands all around, and it was Joe, Samse and Mitch who rode off, heading for Texas and peace.

Frank stirred then and said, "Pull some grub and blankets out of the wagon, Otey. I'm burnin' it."

It was a dismal moment, and once the brush was stacked under the wagon and lighted Frank didn't even look at it. To him, a trail boss and the owner of the herd, the burning of the wagon was a gesture of bitter defeat. It was like selling his saddle. From now on he was just another rider, soon to be on the grub line.

They pulled away from the fire, silent. And then, from down in the brush near the creek, a faint voice called, "Don't leave me."

Frank looked at Red, then pulled his horse around, and they went into the brush. They found a man lying there, murmuring something in the darkness. Frank knelt by him and struck a match, and by its flare he saw one of Corb's crew. The man was shot in the side, and his levis and shirt were soaked with blood.

The rider squinted against the match glare and reached out for Frank's hand. "Don't leave me here, Christian. I can't move," he pled.

"Corb'll be back for you," Frank said tonelessly.

The man gripped his hand harder. "He's the one that shot me," he said bitterly. "He'll let me die."

Otey said, "That satisfies everybody then, I reckon."

"You ain't goin' to leave me?" the man whined. "Corb'll come back and put a slug through my head. I wouldn't rush the camp, so he shot me in the back."

The match died, and then there was only the distant light from the wagon. The man had hold of Frank's wrist, his fingers clutching to his last hope.

Frank looked at Red. "Reckon that's true?"

"I reckon," Red said, "Corb'd do it."

Otey said bitterly, "Leave him there, Frank. What the hell do you care? Half an hour ago he was tryin' to kill you!"

"Put me on a horse!" the man said desperately. "I got to get out of here!"

Frank said, "Can you catch another horse, Red? It don't look like we could leave him here."

Minutes later the four of them left the burning wagon and struck out into the night. Frank rode in bleak silence. He had come into this country with a crew, a wagon, a herd, a partner

and a shack, expecting to take over a big leased range. There
was left to him a scattered herd on range he couldn't claim, a
wounded man he couldn't let die and two friends who were
siding him in a hopeless fight. And, to cap it, he was a wanted
man.

Chapter XIII

BEEF ISSUE TO THE INDIANS came once a week, and its color
and excitement brought out most of the whites from the
agency and the garrison. Long before daylight the Indians,
thousands strong, moved from their camp a mile east of the
agency to the slope by the huge issue corrals across the river
and a mile or so from the garrison. Presently the cavalry troop
from the garrison rode out and took their position on the slope
above the corral, and the issue started.

Because the buffalo were gone and the young bucks had
no other way to prove their hunting prowess, they hunted the
cattle like buffalo. A steer would be turned out of the corral,
and a pair of half-naked Cheyennes on their ponies would
take after him. The chase might lead across the river or into
the very parade ground of the fort before the Indians succeeded in downing the steer, his meager family ration for the
week. Afterward the squaws and the children followed him
and butchered the beef where it had been killed. There was
always tension on this day, for the Indians wanted and needed
more food, and the government would not give it to them.

Milabel, having received that morning the permission he
desired from Puckett to offer a reward for Frank Christian,
dead or alive, drifted out with the garrison crowd to watch
the beef issue on the slope. Above the troopers policing the
affair was a line of buckboards and buggies and saddle horses,
and Milabel rode along the line as if he were looking for
somebody.

When he spied Corb in a buckboard with one of his men
Milabel pulled over to him.

Corb's greeting was amiable enough, as one partner to
another. Milabel said, "I want to talk to you."

Corb said to the man beside him, "Drag it, Rob," and then
invited Milabel to share the buckboard seat. This casual meet-

ing between two sworn enemies was remarked by most of the onlookers, but Milabel and Corb were oblivious to their stares.

Milabel pulled out a sack of dust and rolled a smoke with his huge fists and, after lighting it, said, "Puckett says all right."

"Good," Corb grunted. "We'll see the agent after the issue. I'll put up five hundred of that. We're partners, ain't we?"

Milabel nodded and they fell silent. Corb resumed his study of a young puncher he had been watching for the past few minutes. The puncher was alone, seated cross-legged on the ground, the reins of his horse trailing behind him. He was dressed in ragged clothes, and the expression on his face was proud, a little bit wary and somewhat resentful as he watched the issue.

Corb pointed him out to Milabel and said, "Seen him before?"

Milabel studied him carefully a moment and said, "That's one of Christian's crew."

"I thought so," Corb murmured. He was remembering last night. He had not seen this puncher around the wagon when he had talked to Frank. And now the kid looked footloose. Corb's idea suddenly turned to a hunch, and he murmured, "That kid may be worth talkin' to."

Milabel looked at him, puzzled.

"I'll be back," Corb said. He stepped out of the buckboard and strolled over to where Beach was sitting. He stopped beside him, and Beach looked up at him. Corb nodded coolly and murmured, "No payday, kid?"

Beach said, "What's it to you?" in a surly voice and looked away.

"Nothin'. You look out at the pants, is all. Christian findin' it tough to meet his pay roll?"

"Drag it," Beach said.

Corb chuckled. "Sure. I never rammed money down any man's throat." He walked back to the buckboard and sat down again. Below on the slope a wild pair of Cheyenne bucks tried to turn their steer up the slope and into the cavalry troop. They had almost succeeded before a hard-bitten lieutenant, aware that trouble was brewing, pulled out a gun and killed the steer just as it was heading directly for his men. The Indians shouted angrily and shook their fists at the officer, and he laughed at them.

Presently Beach got up and led his horse over closer to

Corb's buckboard. He covertly studied Milabel and Corb, but they ignored him. He kept edging closer to the buckboard, and at last, with an appearance of nonchalance, he drifted over to stand beside Corb.

"Them damn Indians is goin' to get in trouble," he observed to Corb, and Corb nodded gravely. He was going to allow a man his pride, and Beach, at that moment, needed his pride pretty badly.

Beach cleared his throat and said softly, "What did you mean over there when you said you wouldn't ram money down my throat? What money?"

Corb said bluntly, "I changed my mind. Milabel says you're still workin' for Christian."

"I was workin' for him," Beach said bitterly. "I ain't now."

"Have a tangle?" Corb asked.

Beach sneered. "Got sick of hidin'. I pulled out."

"Lookin' for work?"

"Depends."

Corb shrugged, "Riding'?"

"There ain't much money in that," Beach said, watching him closely. "I can get a ridin' job with a dozen outfits."

Corb rubbed his hands together and considered Beach closely. "I think you and me are talkin' about the same thing. Do you want me to say it or do you want to?"

"You say it," Beach murmured.

"I am goin' to run Frank Christian out of the Nations or kill him," Corb said. "It occurs to me that maybe you can help me."

"I reckon I can," Beach said. He was remembering Frank's words to him that morning at the stampede, fighting words. No man was going to get away with calling him a sheepherder's pup, not any man.

Corb said, "There'll be a 'dead or alive' reward on Christian's head pretty soon. I'll help you collect it and give you the men to do it. How does that sound?"

Beach hesitated, now that the proposition was put to him so bluntly. He looked at the pair of them on the buckboard seat. Milabel's face didn't bother to hide his contempt, and in Corb's eyes was a sort of irony that looked to Beach as if it were partly doubt.

He said as casually as he could, "Sounds like money to me."

"Can you find him?" Corb asked thinly. "Remember, he's on the dodge now and wild as a deer."

Beach considered this, dragging the toe of his worn boot

through the grass and staring at it. Suddenly his boot ceased moving, and he looked up at Corb. "You ain't particular where this shoot-up takes place, are you?"

"No. It'll be legal."

Beach smiled wickedly. "Sure, I can find him for you."

Luvie Barnes came out of the sutler's store at the garrison in midafternoon and nodded to the men on the porch. They tipped their hats to her, and she got her horse at the tie rail, mounted and rode out toward home, a package under her arm. She was halfway down the slope to the river when she heard a horse behind her.

When it pulled alongside her and a voice said, "Afternoon, Miss Barnes," Luvie turned in her saddle to see Scott Corb riding beside her. Luvie was impressed by Corb, not by his appearance as much as by the memory of her father's tales of him. She said, "Good afternoon," with respect.

Corb commented on the weather and gossiped a moment about the garrison, but he was not long in coming to the point, and it was done in an unusually blunt fashion.

"Miss Barnes," he said finally, "I'm goin' to tell you some things and I want your opinion of 'em."

"Of what, Mr. Corb?"

"Last night my riders and myself were held up on Paymaster Creek by two men. A fight resulted, and four of my men are dead this morning. Several days ago a Circle R herd on the north fork was stampeded and a rider shot down in cold blood—by those same two men. It's got to the place now where no rider is safe in this country with those two men loose." He looked at Luvie. "You know who those two men are?"

"No," Luvie said in a small voice.

"Frank Christian and Red Shibe," Corb said.

"No!" Luvie said quickly. "I don't believe that!"

"You've got to believe it," Corb said, "because you can't dodge a fact."

"And you want my opinion on what?"

"How to catch 'em."

Luvie shook her head, her blue eyes troubled. "But I haven't any. How are any criminals caught—if they are criminals?"

"You doubt it?"

"Petty criminals, maybe, and troublemakers. But Frank Christian isn't a murderer."

"You know him, then?"

"I've—seen him, yes."

"At your house?"

Luvie looked sharply at him. "Yes. Why are you so interested?"

"Because you're goin' to help us catch him," Corb said.

Luvie pulled her horse up, her face surprised and angry. "I am? Even if I could, I wouldn't, Mr. Corb! What ever gave you the idea I'd help you?"

"I had a hunch," Corb said, "that you are more or less interested in your dad stayin' in the beef-contractin' business."

"I am," Luvie said slowly. Her eyes were frightened, and Corb saw it.

He made a swift gesture of dismissal with his hand. "Miss Barnes, I don't like to do this. But you'd better know some facts. Frank Christian is trying to kill me, ruin me. He's committed a dozen crimes that he could be arrested for, and against other people besides me. I have a way with these Indians, and if I give them the word they can make trouble for your dad. And if you don't want trouble for your dad, then you'll help me arrest Frank Christian." He smiled faintly. "It's not as if I asked you to commit a crime. I'm asking you to help the law."

"But I don't know where Frank is."

"Edith Fairing does. She can find him for you."

"Then why don't you go to her?"

"Because," Corb said, "she won't do it. And you've got to —unless you're willing to ruin your father."

Luvie didn't say anything for a long moment, watching Corb. This is what she had been afraid of since the very first, what she had warned her father against. And now that it was here she felt only an anger against Frank Christian. But much as she hated him, she couldn't turn him over to the law to be tried for murder.

Corb was shrewd enough so that it wasn't hard for him to imagine what she was thinking, and he saw it was time for him to act.

"Miss Barnes," he said gently, "nobody likes to be known as an informer, least of all a lady like you. But let me ask you some questions. Did you know that there are at least a thousand outlaws in the Nations and that most of them are wanted for murder?"

"Yes."

"And did you know that neither the Indians nor the army

nor the agency have made any attempt to bring them to justice?"

"Yes."

"Then why should the army or the Indians or myself want to bring Frank Christian to trial for murder?"

"But you just said——"

"I said he was *guilty* of murder," Corb said flatly. "If he's caught he won't be tried for murder. He'll be tried for whisky peddling. He'll get out on bond, be tried in Kansas and fined about the price of his bond. There'll be no mention of murder. We're only trying to get him out of the way and fine him." He smiled genially. "Now does that make my blackmail seem pretty reasonable?"

"Are you telling me the truth, Mr. Corb?"

"There's one way to find out," Corb said. "Look around you. In the post office, in Murphy's Hotel. There's reward dodgers for Christian all over the post and the agency. They want him for jail break, not murder. They're not 'dead or alive' dodgers, Miss Barnes."

"But they will be if I don't help you catch him?"

Corb nodded.

"And Dad will have trouble with the Indians if I don't help you?"

Again Corb nodded. Luvie didn't say anything, and Corb went on. "I've been by your house often. You don't have a lamp in the front window. The night Frank Christian comes, in answer to the note you send him through Edith Fairing, you put the lamp in the window. I'll have a man watching. Frank will be arrested then by an army detail. I'll have a man watching for a week, starting tonight." He touched his hat and bid her good-by and pulled his horse around.

In Darlington Luvie turned off on the street that Edith Fairing lived on.

Chapter XIV

IT WAS CLOSE TO SIX O'CLOCK the next night when the fever broke and Corb's rider opened his eyes. Frank and Red were standing over him, watching him, and Frank said, "Want a drink?"

The man nodded, and Frank went over to the seep with a cup. They were camped scarcely two miles from the burned wagon, for Corb's rider had fainted dead away after they put him on a horse.

Frank and Red had stayed with him the whole day while Otey rode into the garrison during the afternoon for advice from the army surgeon. It had been a day of uneasiness, and they took turns sleeping, for both Red and Frank believed Corb's attack of last night would be followed by a man hunt today of the combined crews of Corb and Milabel.

Frank was giving the wounded man a drink when Otey rode into the thicket where they were hiding.

Otey threw down a bottle of medicine and looked at the rider. "How you feelin'?"

"Bad."

"That's good," Otey said. He gestured to the bottle. "I filled it with rattlesnake poison, just in case you don't die."

Red grinned at him, but Otey didn't grin back. For the first time since they had hit the Nations Otey was without work. He had watched while Red and Frank pulled them deeper and deeper into trouble, and now, when fighting was necessary for life, they were saddled with this bum of Corb's, who was better off dead.

Otey sat down and looked at the long slanting sun and contemplated the prospect of a cold supper. He reached in his pocket for his tobacco, and when he pulled it out a piece of folded paper came with it.

Otey picked it up and extended it to Frank. "I almost forgot. Edith Fairing give me that at the agency."

Frank opened it and read it and said to Red, "It's from Luvie Barnes. She says her father's in trouble."

"Who ain't?" Otey said.

"What kind of trouble?" Red asked.

Frank shrugged, staring at the note. He wished he knew himself. It must be bad trouble if Barnes would call on him, for Barnes knew he couldn't be much help. He folded the note and tucked it in his pocket, and his glance settled on the wounded man. He realized immediately that Otey shouldn't have mentioned either Edith's or Luvie's name. He said quietly, "You're likely to hear a lot of things, mister, that your boss would like to hear. Only when you're fit to ride we're shovin' you out of the country."

"That's the best news I've heard," the wounded man said wryly. He was a Texas man, short, lean and with a pockmarked, unshaven face whose pallor made his beard stubble seem also blue.

Frank rose and said to Red, "Well, I reckon we better go see what it is."

The wounded man cut in. "You know the handwritin' of this Barnes girl?"

Frank scowled at him. "What's it to you?"

"It's nothin' to me. It might be to you. Corb could toll you into a bushwhack with a note."

"Not this note!" Red cut in almost angrily. "Edith Fairing gave it to Otey."

"All right, all right," the wounded man said. "I'm just tryin' to help you."

Frank said softly, "What's your name, mister?"

"Call me Gus."

"Thanks for the tip, Gus," Frank said. "It's one to remember." He frowned. "I don't savvy it, though. What's it gettin' you to help us?"

A little color crept into the wounded man's pallid face. "Just put it down to hatin' Corb," he said and looked away.

They had a cold supper of pan bread and jerky, and afterward Otey announced that he would ride into town with Frank. He looked at Red as he said it, but Red didn't protest.

At dark Otey and Frank left the seep and caught up their horses and headed for Darlington. Frank wasn't quite sure why he was going, once he was on his way. Luvie Barnes had first angered him, then called him a fool, then stolen back his bail money, then objected to her father having anything to do with him. There was no reason why he should help her. He wasn't, he reflected, for hadn't she written that her father was in trouble? If she was ever in trouble she'd better not come to him, he thought grimly.

They arrived in Darlington in the middle of the evening, rode through it and tied their horses in the deep shadow of the cottonwood in Barnes's yard. Frank exercised the same caution Red had in approaching the house, but once he was sure there were no visitors he and Otey mounted the porch. He knocked on the door, and it was answered by Luvie.

At sight of him she gave a distinct start and involuntarily put her hand to her mouth in a gesture of dismay.

Noting it, Frank said, "Not much sense in screamin'. You asked me to come, didn't you?"

"Yes, yes," Luvie said in a faint voice. "Step inside." Her dismay seemed to increase at sight of Otey. She was wearing a print dress of maroon silk, and Frank wondered if the contrast made her face so pale.

She said, "Come into the parlor."

Silently Frank and Otey tramped after her. She gestured to the sofa and walked across the room to stand beside the lamp on the table.

Frank said, "Where's Barnes?"

"He'll be back in a little while," Luvie said in an uncertain voice. Then she asked suddenly, "Is it true, Frank, that you killed four of Scott Corb's riders last night?"

Frank smiled crookedly. "So that's got around by now?"

"Is it true?"

Otey said, "Not exactly. Four and a half."

At Luvie's frown Frank explained, "One man's hurt. We're takin' care of him."

Luvie's face suddenly took on a determined cast, and she said coldly, "I suppose you're going to nurse him back to health so you can kill him too?"

Nothing was changed, Frank reflected. Each time they met it was like this. He said, "No, not right away. We figured to fatten him up and eat him for Thanksgiving."

Luvie stamped her foot. "How can you joke about things like that!"

"Joke?" Frank asked in mock surprise. "We're not jokin'. You ought to see his drumsticks."

There was something close to hatred in Luvie's eyes as she looked at him. She reached for the lamp, lifted it off the big table and set it on the low table in front of the window.

"Sit down, please," she said. "Dad's meeting a herd. He'll be back shortly."

Frank sat down on the sofa, Otey in a chair. Frank asked, "What kind of trouble is this?"

"I don't know," Luvie said, sitting down in the rocking chair with her back to the door. "Something you've caused, I suppose."

Frank glared at her and she glared back. She kept plucking a pleat in her skirt, and there was a faint smile on her lips. "Tell me, Frank," she asked, "have you ever been in jail?"

"You ought to know," Frank answered.

Luvie smiled. "Oh, I don't mean a jail you can break out of. I mean one where they have a guard outside your cell door for months and months."

"No."

"Would you like it?"

Frank uncrossed his legs and leaned forward, his gaze wary. "This sounds like you're trying to sell me somethin'," he drawled. "Don't tell me you want me to go back to jail."

"Oh, but I do," Luvie said, her voice sweet with sarcasm.

Otey grunted. Frank leaned back on the sofa, crossing his legs, his mouth a grim line. He gave up. There was no use trying to be decent to her, and once he had the debt paid back to her father—a debt he was certain she had saddled him with—then he wouldn't see any more of them. He cursed the day he ever tried to buy corn and met her.

Luvie had her head cocked as if she was listening. Frank couldn't hear anything, but Luvie rose, saying, "Maybe that's Dad. He's so——"

Crash!

The glass of the front window jangled down on the lamp and at the same time a slug slapped into the wall by Frank's ear. His move was swift, automatic. He rolled over on his side, palming up his gun, and as it exploded the lamp winked out. He yelled at Otey, "Lock the back door!" and rose and swept Luvie to the floor just as the whole night outside opened up in a bedlam of gunfire.

Otey's footsteps hammered down the hallway, and crouching low, Frank ran to the front door, slipped the bolt and crawled back into the parlor. He put a hand out and touched Luvie's shoulder and it was shaking. He said, "Are you hurt?"

Then he heard her sobs, and she spoke to him. "Oh, Frank, what have I done, what have I done!"

"Done?" Frank echoed blankly. "Nothin'. It's what they're doin'."

"But I did it, Frank!" Luvie moaned. "It's Corb! He was going to have the army arrest you tonight! That note was to bring you here! That lamp in the window was to tell them you were here!"

Frank lay there, not believing his ears. The rifle fire poured in both the parlor windows, chipping the wall in a line a foot above their heads.

"I can see it now!" Luvie sobbed. "It was a trap to kill you! And I led you into it!"

Frank said at last, "Yeah," in a low, bitter voice. "That's about it."

"You can't let them, Frank! You can't! I don't care if

Corb ruins Dad! I'll do anything to get you out of this, anything!"

Frank said as gently as he could, "Then quit cryin'. I know you hate me, Luvie, but I——"

"But I don't!" Luvie cried. "I—I've found that out in this last minute." She put a hand out to Frank. "Corb said you were murdering his riders, Frank. You even admitted it tonight, and I had to go through with it then. He said he only wanted to arrest you and get you out of the way! He said the army would do it! This isn't the army! It's murder!"

"Quiet," Frank said. He was trying desperately to think. From over in the corridor Otey called grimly, "They've surrounded the place, Frank. When they rush us we're done for."

Frank didn't answer. He was still thinking. He had to get Luvie Barnes out of here, and Otey had to go with her. Otey, like the loyal hand he was, would be shot down in a quarrel that wasn't his own. And one more man wouldn't make any difference now in defending this place.

Frank touched Luvie's hand. "Can you hear me?"

"Yes."

"You've got to get out of here. I'll call to——"

"But I won't," Luvie said passionately. "I wish they'd shoot me! I wish I could die!"

Frank said savagely, "Dammit, girl! You're worth more out there than in here! Now listen. Otey's goin' with you. They haven't got anything against him. When he gets out have him ride to your dad's herd and warn him to be on the lookout, because Corb will raid it if I break loose."

"But how can you, Frank? How can you?"

"I'll get away," Frank said above the rifle fire. "All you got to do is get out there and keep Corb from burning this place down on top of me. You understand that?"

"Yes," Luvie said weakly.

Frank felt Otey crawl up beside him. Otey asked, "You aim to fight it out, Frank?"

"That's right," Frank said. "I'll have Corb let her out, and then let 'em take us if they can."

"Suits me," Otey said briefly.

The rifle fire slacked off a little, and Frank raised up and bawled, "Corb! Corb!"

The rifle fire dribbled off, and from out in the yard Corb's voice answered, "Christian?"

"There's a woman in here!" Frank called. "Hold your fire till she gets out!"

"Send her out!" Corb called. He yelled orders to his men to hold their fire.

Frank rose and helped Luvie up. "Unlock the front door, Otey," Frank said, and as Otey vanished into the hall Frank pulled Luvie toward the door.

Otey had the door open a foot, peering out into the dark night. Off near the corrals someone had built a fire that was dying. There were noises from the town beyond, noises of shouting, of people running to see what was happening.

Otey said bitterly, "They're goin' to nail us in front of the crowd, Frank. Damn 'em!"

He pulled his head back in, and then Frank lashed down with his gun barrel. It caught Otey behind the ear, and he melted to the floor without a word. Luvie gasped, and Frank said quickly, "I've got to get him out of here, Luvie, and he wouldn't leave me unless I made him. Can you carry him? He's light."

"I'll try," Luvie said.

Frank took Otey's gun and shell belt and strapped them on himself, then he caught Otey under the arms, hoisted him, and Luvie put one of Otey's arms around her shoulder. Otey wasn't much of a load, and Luvie said, "I can do it, Frank."

Frank raised his voice. "Here she comes, Corb!"

"All right."

Luvie said to Frank, "You've got to get out, Frank! You've got to! I'll—kill myself if you don't!"

And without waiting for him to answer she stepped out onto the porch, half dragging, half carrying Otey.

Frank locked the door and went back into the parlor, and through the shattered window he followed her progress across the yard toward the cottonwoods. Nobody shot. She was received by two men who lighted matches to examine the burden she was carrying. She refused to give Otey up, and they let her pass, and then the firing started again.

Frank crawled back in the hall and considered what to do next. Certain there was only one man in the house, they would be sure to rush the place. Behind that knowledge, Frank wondered how Corb would dare to do it. This house was almost in town. A hundred people would watch it, and somebody was bound to stop him. You didn't hunt a man down and kill him for jail break. But they were, he thought bitterly, thanks to Luvie.

He crawled back into the corridor and heard a savage hammering on the back door. He couldn't defend the whole house. Then he'd better defend part of it. If Luvie could stop Corb from burning the house, then he could hold the second floor until the army got here and stopped the massacre. He lunged for the stairway in the hall just as the back door crashed open. He achieved the second-story landing as a pair of Corb's riders broke through the front door and ran for the stairs.

Lying on his belly, Frank fanned one gun empty down the stair well, and the two men rolled back down on the floor. Then, from the front doorway, two riflemen started pouring shots at the landing, and Frank had to crawl back. But not before he saw three riders, bellies flattened to the steps, coming up under the withering barrage from the doorway.

He backed off down the second-story hall. There was a window at each end, the front one looking out onto the sloping porch roof, the rear framing a segment of night sky.

He took up his position under the front window. If nobody got up the stairs, then nobody could get him. When the first dark figure appeared above the stair well Frank shot, and he heard the sound of a body tumbling down the stairs and a chorus of soft curses. Corb's men were waiting there almost at the top of the steps, unable to go further and unwilling to risk his withering fire from the hall.

There was a bedlam of activity belowstairs. He could hear Corb cursing out his men, ordering them up the stairs, and the flat refusal of the men to commit suicide. Corb gave orders for ladders to be got and the second-story windows stormed, and there were objections to that. And then, cutting in on the talk, was Luvie's cool voice. She was here, she said, to see that they didn't burn the place down, seeing that all decency had been forgotten and that Corb had gone back on his word. The voices of a couple of townsmen bore her out.

While this interminable argument was in progress, and Corb getting more and more bitter, Frank was crouched down below the hall window, his eyes glued to the dark stair well.

And then, from out in the yard, came the sound of a

horse galloping toward the house. The arguing below was stilled, and then the horse stopped and a loud voice demanded, "Where's Corb?"

"Here," Corb called. Frank could hear him walking toward the porch.

"Captain Haggard, Corb," the man said angrily. "What in the hell is going on here?"

"What do you think?" Corb asked.

"That you've got Frank Christian cornered here and are trying to down him!"

"That's right," Corb said.

"On whose authority? Christian is wanted by the agency for whisky peddling and jail break, and the agency doesn't want a corpse. Call your men off and keep Christian cornered until I can get some men here! Damn you, Corb, you're not the army or the police!"

Corb's steps went out onto the edge of the porch. "Did the major send you?"

"No. I was in the officers' bar when word came. But I've a right to demand the agency's prisoner."

"He's not your prisoner," Corb said grimly. "He's fair game. Go down to the Murphy Hotel and read the notice that was printed this afternoon and put up an hour ago. It's a 'dead or alive' reward, Captain. With the agent's permission."

There was a long pause. "If you're lying to me, Corb, I'll see you in jail!"

"Go back and read it, Captain," Corb taunted. "When you get back with your soldiers Christian will be dead!"

Frank, knowing now why Corb dared to corner him in town, rose to look out over the slanting porch roof. The captain's voice seemed to be coming from almost under it. The window was open, and Frank stepped out onto the porch roof, and then he was sure of it. The captain was pulled up by the porch steps. Quietly Frank holstered his guns and inched his way down the slippery shingles.

He heard the captain say, "If he is dead, you'll pay through the nose, Corb."

There was jangling of the bridle chain and the muffled sound of a shod horse turning on hard-packed ground. Frank, hunkered down on the edge of the porch roof, his boots slowly slipping, saw a dark form pull out from beneath him.

"All right!" Corb shouted to his men. "Up the stairs!"

Frank leaped then. He arced out from the porch, feet

first, at the moving horse below him. He landed astride the horse's rump just behind the saddle, and the horse almost went down, caught itself and came up.

Frank wrapped his arms around the captain and yanked him over to one side, pulling him out of the saddle.

The captain yelled, "Corb!" and then Frank brought up his fist in a tight arc that ended behind the captain's ear. He slumped out of the saddle, and Frank grabbed at the reins as the horse reared and Corb yelled, "Out here, you fools! Out here!" and shot.

Frank fought the horse down, then, lying low across his neck, roweled him savagely. The horse streaked off in the darkness, and the crowd hanging back on the edge of the yard began to shout. One man shot, and then it was taken up by others. Frank headed for the cottonwoods. A horse-man loomed out of the darkness shooting, and Frank palmed up his gun and shot blindly. His horse rammed into the other horse, stumbled, and Frank pulled him up. Now the whole night was alive with shooting, and Frank prayed for the shelter of the barn. He achieved the corner of it just as a dozen slugs slapped into the timber at the corner, and he was safe.

He dodged the horse around the corral, jumped him over the watering trough and then sent him into the trees and pulled him over at right angles and headed off through the timber. Already close behind him was the sound of the first of his pursuers.

The army had grain-fed horses, Frank remembered, and he smiled. They'd have to ride hard to catch him tonight, let alone set eyes on him. And next time there wouldn't be a traitorous woman to betray him.

Chapter XV

FRANK, hungry and dog tired from covering up his trail so thoroughly that even the Indian trackers from the post couldn't follow him, spotted Barnes's herd next noon. It had been thrown off the Chisholm and was being loose-herded on the flats beside a feeder creek of the Canadian, some eighteen miles below the post. The fact that the cattle were being loose-herded was proof enough that Otey had reached Barnes with the word to be on guard, but if he needed more proof there was the tent beside the chuck wagon. The army quartermaster never received herds this far out from the post, so the tent could mean only one thing. They were waiting for him.

He put his horse out of the timber, and the first rider saw him and pulled up to wait for him. Frank identified himself, and they started out together for the tent. It was a warm spring day with the tall grass stirring under the fitful wind, and Barnes's herd looked well fleshed. His own steers would be taking on flesh now, Frank thought bitterly, and then he put it out of his mind. There were other things to worry about.

Approaching the tent, the rider gave a hail. Out of the tent poured Otey, Barnes and Red. Red let out a whoop of joy that made the grazing cattle raise their heads in lazy inquiry, and then Frank slipped out of the McClellan saddle and confronted them.

Red pounded him on the back, and Otey, for once unable to talk, pumped his hand while Barnes pumped the other one. And then Frank caught sight of Luvie in the tent door. Her face was unsmiling as she came toward him, and she was biting her lower lip.

She stopped before him and said, "I guess there's no use telling you how sorry I am, Frank."

"No, I don't reckon there's any use," Frank said. "It wouldn't do any good."

Luvie said, "But there in the house you said it didn't matter."

"What I said in the house and what I say here are two different things," Frank murmured, no anger in his voice. "I agreed with you in the house so I could get you out of there. I don't have to agree with anything out here. You're free. So am I. It's quits."

"Frank," Luvie said, "I'm sorry."

"I heard you."

"I'll make it up to you any way I can."

"There ain't any way," Frank said. "You tolled me to the house so Corb could take me. It just happened you believed he didn't aim to kill me, only jail me. You did it because you wanted to help your dad. All right, I believe you. Let's let it ride."

"But, Frank, I'm not like that! I wouldn't——"

"You're sorry for yourself," Frank said. "You're scared every time you think what might have happened. You'll get over it, though. And you'll pull some knotheaded trick again to get me into trouble, like stealin' your dad's bail money. The only difference is I won't bite on a note again. Get it through that pretty little head of yours that I'm tryin' to help your dad, not you. He was kind to me once and got in a jam for it. I'll try to get him out of it—if you'll keep out of it!"

"Easy, boy," Barnes said, his voice troubled. "She's sorry. Don't rub it in so." He came over to stand by Luvie, and she put her small hand in his. There was humiliation and grief in her face, and she didn't meet Frank's eyes.

"Sure," Frank said, his eyes glinting. "She's sorry. She's pretty too, and I'd like to see more of her. Only I can't crowd my luck much further, so I better quit seein' her before I'm carried out on a shutter."

Luvie made a small gesture with her hand. "I deserve it all, Frank. Thanks for telling me." And she turned and went into the tent. Gus, lying on a cot inside the tent after his forced ride of last night, waved to Frank and Frank nodded to him. Barnes went in with Luvie, murmuring something, and Frank walked over to Red and Otey.

"You can be a tough devil, Frank," Red murmured.

Frank's eyes were still smoldering. He looked at Red and nodded. "You'd be tough, too, if she'd invited a whole town in to shoot at you."

Barnes came out then, his face troubled. He mopped his brow and came up to Frank, shaking his head. "I'm sorry you feel about Luvie the way you do, Frank."

"Listen," Frank said, anger making his voice ominous. "I don't feel any way about Luvie, Barnes! Let's don't talk about her again. I'd like to help you, because you're the only man in this whole damn Nations that tried to help me. I pay back my debts. If you don't like it, I can ride out of here."

"Forget it, forget it," Barnes said mildly. He looked around him. "There's some shade by the wagon. Let's talk over there."

They filed over to the chuck wagon and sat down in the grass. Frank pulled a hay stem and chewed on it, and for a long moment there was an awkward silence.

Otey broke it. "Well, Corb's done all he can to Frank, Barnes. It looks like you're in for it. He warned Luvie, and I reckon he'll carry out his threat."

"I don't mind losin' a herd," Barnes said grimly. "I want a crack at him."

"You won't get it," Red said.

"Why not?"

"You tell him, Frank," Red said. "I reckon you've got it figured out the same way I have."

Frank nodded. "The Indians'll work on you. Not him."

"Unh-hunh," Barnes said in thoughtful assent. "Another raid."

"Only this time they'll shoot. They'll pick a fight, kill as many men as they can and scatter your herd from hell to breakfast."

"You think so?" Barnes said, his eyes suddenly alert. "Why?"

"I'll tell you why," Frank said grimly. "I've seen this thing buildin' up, Barnes. Corb is safe here just as long as he can keep cattlemen like me under his thumb. He's made a couple of tries for me and he's missed. And there are fifty trail bosses and small cattlemen that are watchin' me, hopin' I'll win and knowin' for certain I won't. If I knock Corb over, they'll swarm into these reservations, and Corb won't be able to stop 'em. So he's got to down me, and now he's got to down you too, because you helped me. You understand that much of it?"

Barnes nodded, his intent gaze on Frank's face.

"Then he's got to use his Indians," Frank said.

"Why?"

Frank said, "Because he's got to lick you, and he figures that's the one thing you can't fight. You'll be scared to, because if you fight them we got an Indian uprising on our hands."

Barnes didn't say anything for a full half minute. "It's like that, eh?" he murmured, and Frank nodded.

None of them spoke for a while, for they realized without having to put it into words what it meant. It meant a pack of whisky-filled, murdering Cheyennes on the warpath. It meant that every white man, woman and child would have to seek the protection of the garrison, and it meant that additional troops from the Department of the Missouri would be sent out to reinforce Fort Reno. It meant days and nights of fighting, of pillage, of anxious hours of waiting, before white supremacy was once again established. And it meant building from the ground up everything that had been done on the reservation. It was this last thought that prompted Otey to say, "It's been comin' to a head for years. Maybe if it happens, this country can start out with a clean slate."

"Without coyotes like Corb," Red murmured.

Barnes's honest face was puzzled. He was trying to reduce all this to its simplest terms.

"You mean," he said finally, "I got to let Corb shoot up my crew and steal my cattle through them tame Indians of his, and if I fight him I'm liable to start an Indian war?"

"That's it," Frank said.

Barnes's jaw clamped shut with a click. "I'm an American in an honest business, I reckon. And I'll fight for it. I ain't the one that let Corb come in here and buy his Indians with whisky. I ain't the one that's half starved these Indians until they're mean. And I ain't the one that's let things get to such a hell of a state that an honest man can't speak his mind." He looked at Frank. "I'll fight."

"Remember what it means," Frank said.

"I know what it means!" Barnes said. "Hell, I fought Comanches half my life. I'll fight these damn Cheyennes the other half of it!"

"It might be a match that'll touch off the whole powder keg," Frank said.

Barnes stood up, his face red. "That suits me too."

Red came to his feet. "Hell, we may be invitin' trouble," he said. "But if we can save this herd, let's do it."

It was Frank who pointed out that the Indians, following age-old custom of their race, were not night fighters. So if there was a raid on the cattle it would be this afternoon, for by night driving the herd could be in the government-issue corrals by daylight tomorrow morning.

Barnes nodded, walked out and bawled to the nearest rider, "Ed, bring the boys in!"

When the whole crew of eight men was gathered around the chuck wagon Barnes told them what was expected. The statement that they might have to fight the Indians brought a smile from every man in the crew. As trail men they had suffered long and patiently under the insolence of the Indians who demanded beef for the use of the trail through their reservations. But a stern government, fearing Indian trouble, had forbidden them to retaliate. This now was an invitation to settle an old grudge, and not a man accepted Barnes's offer to ride off with full pay.

"Then scatter and keep watch. At sunset throw the herd together and we'll start the drive," Barnes said.

Afterward Frank took a blanket and slept under the wagon during the long uneasy afternoon when everyone else in camp, Luvie included, mounted guard.

An hour before dark the cook called supper for half the watch. Frank was wakened and ate with the first shift. Barnes and Luvie were both absent, and Frank wolfed down his food along with the silent crew, anxious to avoid her. Halfway through eating, Frank remembered Gus and took a plate of food and started for the tent. As he entered he saw Gus standing up, drawing his knees high in experiment. When Gus heard Frank he wheeled, and they peered at each other in the half gloom of the tent.

"Here's some grub," Frank said.

Gus took it, nodding his thanks, and Frank started out again.

"Frank."

Frank paused and regarded him.

"That still hold about you shovin' me out of the Nations soon's I can ride?"

"It holds."

"I can ride," Gus said. "Tonight."

"How's your side?"

"All right. Good enough to ride. I want to."

Frank nodded and went back to the fire. Most of the crew had ridden out to relieve the others, but Frank stayed until Barnes and Luvie and Red and Otey rode in to eat. Luvie didn't look at him. She was quiet, her face sad, and she unsmilingly accepted Red's small attentions to her. Barnes took a tin plate, filled it with grub and sat down to eat beside her.

Frank came up alongside him and squatted by him. "Can I buy a horse from you, Barnes?"

"Nope," Barnes said, his mouth full. "I'll give you one."

"It's for Gus. He's headin' back for Texas."

The horse wrangler, who had brought in the remuda, was eating across the fire, and Barnes called to him to saddle an extra horse. Frank should have gone then, but he wanted to make sure Gus left. Presently Gus came out with his empty plate, drank a cup of coffee standing in the shadows, then looked at Frank.

The horse wrangler came up, leading a hammerheaded blue roan carrying a worn-out saddle with a sack of grub tied behind the cantle.

Frank boosted Gus into the saddle, and Gus bit his bloodless lip to keep from crying out. But once he was in the saddle the pain eased out of his face.

"You can stay if you don't think you'll make it," Frank said.

"I'll make it," Gus said.

Frank stepped back. "All right. My promise is still good. If I lay eyes on you in this country again I'll hunt you down like I would a lobo."

Gus nodded, his curious gaze on Frank's face. He licked his lips, looked over at Red, who was watching, then looked back at Frank.

"Me and that redhead couldn't sleep last night," Gus said slowly. "We got to talkin', and he asked some questions."

Frank frowned and looked over at Red, who was staring intently at Gus.

"You was Morg Wheelon's partner, wasn't you?" Gus said to Frank.

"Yes," Frank said slowly.

"Anyone told you that when Morg was found he had a busted hand, like he'd been in a fight?"

Frank nodded.

"He was in a fight," Gus stated. "Out by the corral where they found him."

"How do you know?" Frank asked swiftly.

Gus smiled faintly. "You want to hear this or don't you?"

"Go on."

"Morg knocked this ranny down. Knocked him against the poles. This fella's spur caught between them two cedar anchor posts for the gate. It jammed there when he tried to get up. Morg hit him so hard then that the spur broke, and he went rollin' off under a horse. The man ridin' the horse had a shotgun across his lap. This fella grabbed the shotgun and killed Morg."

"Who was it?"

Gus shook his head. "Find out. He's had the spur patched and he's wearin' it. And the broke piece is still at the corral unless somebody found it. Find the broke piece, find the patched spur, and if they match you've got your killer."

"Who was it?" Frank said.

Again Gus shook his head. "It won't work, Frank. If I

squeal I'll get a slug." He paused, regarding Frank thoughtfully. "You was good to me. You fed me and took care of me and give me a horse to ride out on when you could have shot me. I've told you as much as I can. You figure out the rest of it." He grinned suddenly and held out a boot. "Take a look at my spurs first. I don't hone for a shot in the back." Frank looked at his spur, and then Gus pulled his horse around and Frank looked at the other. Then Gus touched his hat to Luvie and rode away from the fire in a southerly direction.

Frank started after him, but Red put a hand on his arm. "He won't tell, Frank. It's his neck if he does."

"But how'd he happen to see it?" Frank asked vehemently. "He was there. Who was he workin' for? Corb?"

Red shook his head slowly. "Corb and Milabel. He's took turns workin' for them both. He told me last night."

Frank stared at Red and then slowly relaxed. He had to be content with this one clue, but it was better than none. He shrugged Red's hand off and went out to get his horse. But he did not follow Gus. He headed for the cattle that were being pushed into the big herd preparatory to moving.

The drive that night was a job. Thirsty cattle, with the hope of water ahead, will drive easily at night; but these cattle had been loafed up from Texas, putting on weight each day, and their habits were uneasy and stubborn now, and it took the crew a long time to get them under way back to the Chisholm.

Afterward it was easier. Frank rode point, sometimes with Otey and sometimes with Red, and he could hear snatches of songs the riders were singing at their positions in the swing. In the drag was the chuck wagon, in which Luvie was riding.

The only danger until daylight lay in the possibility of an attack from Corb's white crew, and there was little to fear from that. Corb was too smart to play it that way. And as the tension slacked off Frank cast about for a key to Gus's riddle. Tomorrow, with Barnes's cattle safe, he could go back to the burned shack and find the broken spur point. Red and Otey were free, and if need be they would rope and hog-tie every man at the post and the agency until they found the man. After that—well——Frank wouldn't name it in his own mind.

An hour before dawn Frank realized that they would not complete the drive during darkness. The new grass was still attractive enough to the cattle that they broke away to feed, and the discipline of the crew, short tempered by this time, had them restive and nervous.

When dawn broke and Frank, still riding point, located himself he knew they were far enough away from the agency that they were still in danger. He rose in his stirrups to signal the swing rider to push them harder, and when he turned round again there were riders pulling out of a dip in the land ahead. His heart sank, and he peered through the faint dawn light, and when he had identified them as Indians he wheeled his horse and rode back to Red.

Red had seen them too, and he regarded Frank gloomily.

"I'll pull them over and make medicine with 'em," Frank said quickly. "Whatever happens, don't let 'em split the herd, and keep it movin'. Pass the word back!"

And he set his horse into a gallop and rode up to point position.

The Cheyennes, in a motley array of buckskin and calico shirts with tails flying, must have numbered twenty. They were carrying old muskets, spears, bows and arrows and an occasional repeating rifle, although firearms were barred to them by army decree. They drew up in a line across the path of the cattle and held up their hands, palms out, in a gesture to halt.

Frank dropped back to the lead steer and put his horse against him, gently turning him to one side. As soon as the Cheyennes were certain that he wasn't turning the cattle to mill them, but only to pass their line, they started yelling. Frank quickly pulled away from the lead steer, letting him keep his course, and slanted off for the closest Indian yelling. and the Indians' curiosity pulled them aside. The ruse worked easily, for the Cheyennes were torn between stopping the herd and talking to Frank. To make them more uncertain Frank began to gesture as he approached.

He picked out their leader and rode up to him, and out of the corner of his eye he noted that the first dozen steers had merely walked around the Indian ponies and dropped back to their course. Red had signaled Otey, the swing rider across the herd, to move up, so that he was almost opposite Frank now. Any attempt to split the herd, which was increasing every second in width, would be met by Otey's gun.

Frank turned to the Indian and said in Comanche, "Out of the way!" in a harsh voice.

"Stop the cattle!" the Cheyenne said angrily. "We need meat!"

"Not this meat," Frank answered.

The Indian saw that he had lost the advantage in allowing the lead steers to pass him, and he turned and yelled something at the farthest buck. Frank saw the Indian pull his pony around to head off the leaders, and he knew that he would have to act now.

With the back of his hand he lashed the Indian across the mouth.

"Out of the way!" he yelled.

The whole thing exploded then. The Indians yelled, and one of them let a gun off. Frank roweled his horse into the nearest Indian, palming his gun up and slashing down at his head. The Indian ducked and took it on the shoulder, and far behind Frank heard Red shooting into the air to stampede the cattle. Frank, using his gun like a club, fell into the pack of Indians, slashing his way through them. The range was too close for the Indians to use their rifles, and jammed as they were, on frightened plunging horses, their spears and bows were useless.

The slow thunder of running cattle started then, and Frank knew that the herd could never be split now. One Indian leaped on his back, winding an arm around his neck, and Frank raised his gun blindly by his ear and shot. The Indian's hold relaxed, and there ahead of his, his face contorted in fury, was a buck with his spear raised. Frank yanked his horse into a rear and shot point-blank at the Cheyenne, and he went out of the saddle.

The fringe of the herd was pouring into them now, adding to the panic of the screaming horses and the milling Cheyennes. Ahead of him another buck had fitted an arrow to his bow and was sitting a rearing horse, knees clamped, as he aimed at Frank. The bow twanged and Frank felt a whisper past his ear, and then he shot and the Indian was driven off his pony to be trampled on by three panicked steers.

Frank was clear of them now and, leaning low over his horse's neck, he roweled him into the open and raced alongside the running steers. There was a scattering of shots, and a steer beside him stumbled and went down. Frank looked back over his shoulder. The Indians were fighting savagely to get their horses out of the way of the onstreaming steers, and beyond them Red and two riders, both guns blazing, were riding them down. Only half the Indians seemed to be mounted now, and the free horses were adding to the confusion.

Frank settled down to fast riding now. Up ahead and across the herd, Otey was riding. Frank's horse stretched into a long gallop over the level plain, creeping up on the leaders. Otey, catching sight of Frank when he pulled abreast him across the herd, yelled something, but Frank motioned him on. As soon as Frank outdistanced the leader he swung over toward Otey, and they were riding side by side.

"Ride for the issue corral and get the gates open!" Frank yelled. "I'll try to turn them!"

Otey nodded and whipped up his horse, and Frank dropped back beside the lead steers. He had changed places with Otey now, taking the right side of the herd. Back of him the ominous steady thunder of the stampeding cattle was like a sword over his head. One slip of his horse and he was under these thousand hooves which would cut him to ribbons. The dust the herd was raising blotted out sight behind, so that Frank could only guess at the outcome of the fight. But he knew that the cattle would follow each other blindly and that they would all follow the leaders. Barnes's herd had not been split.

They were off the flat now, on the long downslope toward the north fork. Off to the left was Darlington, and Frank could see Otey streaking across the flat below and disappearing down the riverbank. On the opposite slope, far up to the left, the issue corrals were visible.

Frank had to turn the leaders soon, and he glanced down at the lead steer. He was running with a glassy-eyed panic, lost to anything except fright. Frank stayed by him until they hit the river. As luck would have it, it was a low bank, and the steers poured over it and into the great sandy bed of the river. The sand slowed them down a little but not much. Frantically Frank reloaded his gun and held it in his left hand, waiting his chance.

The opposite bank was steeper, and the lead steer slowed down as he climbed it, the others behind him lunging into the pull too. Frank gauged his chance carefully.

When the lead steer reached the very top of the bank, at his slowest speed, Frank fired his gun almost in the steer's face. The steer pulled away from the noise, running again, but this time slanting in the direction of the corrals. The others followed blindly.

Frank could see the corrals up ahead. Otey was opening the six gates that swung inward into the big corrals. Frank gauged the direction of the steer's travel, saw that it was not

yet right and fired his gun again. And again the lead steer
swung to the left and the others followed.

Satisfied, Frank holstered his gun and reined away, for
he would have to get out of the way of the herd in their mad
rush and ride out before he was seen. His horse rammed into
something, and Frank lifted his glance from the lead steer.
The other steers had caught up with the leader and were
running abreast of him in a long line.

Frank poured leather into his horse, but the horse was too
tired to bring up any extra speed. For ten bleak seconds
Frank tried to push him ahead and away from the herd, but
the horse couldn't do it. They were close to the yawning
gates of the corral now, and Frank knew it was useless. His
only hope was to streak for the other side of the corral and
climb out that way.

The herd swept into the six gates of the corral like a tidal
wave, and Otey, high on the stout gatepost in the middle of
them, yelled something at Frank as he was swept through
too. But Frank only saw his mouth work; the thunder of
the herd drowned out all speech.

Frank roweled his horse, heading for the far fence, but
the horse did not respond. Swiftly the cattle pulled ahead and
closed the way in front of him, and then they met the far
fence and swerved, milling around in a circle and stopping
Frank's headway.

He was in the center of that circle on a spent horse. He
was imprisoned, his horse moving with the tide of the cattle
as they milled around the corral. The nearest fence was two
hundred feet from him, and his horse was helpless to move
in the mass of milling cattle.

Frank fought the horse, trying to pull him toward the
fence, and then pity conquered. The horse had done his best
and he could do no more. Cursing savagely, Frank pulled his
hat low over his face and patiently tried to work his horse
toward the fence. He had got a dozen yards when the head
of the first trooper appeared over the top posts of the corral.
The trooper yelled and pointed, and other troopers joined
him.

Frank hid his face, trying to act like a puncher who now
wanted to break up the milling. He heard shouts, and Otey's
cracked voice was raised in anger. When he looked up again
he saw the top rail of the corral lined with troopers, and they
had their rifles trained on him.

Then the voice of their officer rose above the cattle

bawling. "All right, Christian. We've got you trapped! Throw your gun over!"

And Frank had no choice.

Chapter XVI

BY NOON the word was already around that seven Cheyennes had been killed by trail drivers. The streets of Darlington and the post emptied of Indians as if by magic, and the more timid folk in Darlington, reading the signs, locked their houses and moved across the river to the protection of the garrison. There was much curiosity as to what was going on at the Indian camp downriver, but no white man dared investigate.

Luvie and Red, barred from Fort Reno, went back to the Barnes place with the crew while Otey and Barnes went before the commandant. They were closeted with him all morning while Red paced the yard of Barnes's place and smoked incessantly.

In early afternoon, when Barnes and Otey rode into the place, Red could tell by their grim faces that the session hadn't been a pleasant one. They all filed into the kitchen where Luvie had something to eat for them, and while Barnes ate Otey told the story.

"They got him in a stone guardhouse with five sentries around it. Tonight at midnight they're sneakin' him out of the garrison and makin' a dash to Kansas with him."

"Kansas?" Luvie asked. "Why?"

"For trial, I reckon, and to keep him away from the Indians," Otey said. "They'll slap a dozen more charges on him now."

Luvie turned back to the stove, but not before Red saw that her face was pale and her lips were trembling. She had changed into a light summer dress now and outwardly seemed the most cool and unworried of anyone in the room. Red knew she wasn't, though.

Barnes suddenly shoved his plate away from him in disgust. "When I think," he said bitterly, "that if it wasn't for me wantin' to save that herd Frank would be free now, I feel like cuttin' my throat."

Red, gloomily smoking on the other side of the round kitchen table, said nothing. Otey looked bleakly at him, and for once there was no rancor in his glance. Frank's capture had succeeded in bringing them a tolerance of each other that no good fortune could have affected.

Luvie, at the stove, suddenly wheeled and said in a low, bitter voice, "Why don't we do something, then? We sit around here and do nothing!"

"Do what?" her father asked gloomily.

"I don't know!" Luvie cried. "But look at us! Dad, if it hadn't been for Frank, you'd have lost a herd! Red, if it wasn't for Frank, you'd still be a saddle bum. Otey, if Frank hadn't hit you over the head and got you out of the house during the fight, you'd be dead. And so would I." Her eyes were flashing. "And still we can't do anything now he's in trouble."

"But you can't take a man away from the army!" Barnes exclaimed.

"Why can't you?" Luvie cried.

Nobody spoke for a second, and then Red's eyes came alight for a moment, then died.

Barnes said patiently, "Talk sense, girl. You just can't."

But Luvie had seen Red's eyes. Presently Red got up and walked out to the back porch. He sat on the top step, looking off toward the town.

Luvie came out and sat beside him, not speaking immediately. Then she said, "Red."

Red looked at her.

"I saw your face when I said that."

"Said what?"

"Don't try to hide it, Red. It gave you an idea, didn't it?"

Red nodded slowly. "A loco one."

"Tell me," Luvie said. When Red didn't speak Luvie put a hand on his arm. "Oh, Red, let me help. Can't you see I've got to!"

"I reckon I can," Red said. "You wait here."

Red went back into the kitchen, and Luvie heard him speaking to Otey. Otey came out presently, mounted and rode off in the direction of town.

Red came out and said to Luvie, "Come along."

They got their horses and rode in to Darlington and through the town until they came to the shaded street where Edith Fairing lived. As they approached Edith's house they saw her out in the small corral saddling her horse.

When she saw them she dropped the bridle and called to Red, "Is it true they've caught Frank?"

Red nodded. Edith looked at him a long moment, then said hello to Luvie. Red folded his arms and leaned on the saddle horn. "You ridin' out?"

"I was saddling up to ride over to the Barnes's to ask if it was true about Frank," Edith answered, and then she added, "Is there anything I can do, Red?"

Red didn't answer directly. He asked, "You figure there's anything to this talk about an Indian uprising?"

"I don't know, Red. Why?"

Red looked at her gravely. She was wearing a blue divided skirt and red blouse, and Red noticed for the first time that they were Indian colors, worn the way an Indian would wear them. It encouraged him to go on.

"You reckon anything would happen to a white who rode out to the Cheyenne camp?"

Edith frowned and looked at Luvie, who shrugged almost imperceptibly.

"It would depend on who it was," Edith said.

"You, for instance."

Edith laughed. It was the first time Red had heard her laugh, and he liked it. "Anything happen to me? Red, I was raised with a good many of those Cheyenne and Arapaho bucks. I used to play in their lodges, and when I got tired I would go in and talk to the old warriors about the days when they were moved into the Nations. They were friends with my father, Red. Nothing would happen to me. Why?"

Red's hunch was borne out. Again he didn't answer Edith directly. "Is Stone Bull a good chief, Edith?"

"The best."

Red lapsed into silence, and Edith made an impatient gesture with her hand. "For heaven's sake, Red! What is it?"

"Do you reckon Stone Bull would come with you to the Barnes place tonight if you rode out and asked him?"

"I'm sure he would if I could tell him what it's all about."

"It's about Frank," Red said. He grinned suddenly. "I'd go to the chief, only I reckon they'd lift my hair out there."

"It won't make more trouble, will it, Red?" Edith asked.

"We'll see what Stone Bull says," Red answered. He slipped to the ground, took the bridle from the corral pole and finished saddling Edith's horse while she and Luvie talked.

When Luvie and Red left Edith on the way back to the Barnes place Red was silent. Luvie tried to pry out of Red what it was all about, but Red only shook his head. "Tonight, when Stone Bull comes, you have a two-gallon bucket of tea ready and just listen," Red said. He left her at the house and disappeared toward Darlington.

Both Otey and Red were late for supper, and Barnes was not there at all, for the army was receiving his herd that afternoon and evening and he was busy with the quarter-master. There was an air of suppressed excitement about Red that made Luvie so curious she wanted to shake it out of him, but all she could do was wait.

A little while after dark, when Red and Otey were sitting impatiently around the kitchen table, a knock came on the back door, and Luvie went to answer it. She held the door wide open, and an Indian stepped into the room, Edith following him.

He was an old man, heavy but not fat, and at first glance his face seemed fierce and stern. But there was a quiet un-smiling dignity about him that transcended his dirty collar-less shirt and wrinkled pants. Edith introduced him, and he gravely shook hands with Otey and Red. Luvie, Indian fashion, was ignored.

The three men and Edith sat at the table, and the talk be-gan. Red knew Indian ways well enough to know that half the evening must pass before it would be polite to bring up the main subject of conversation, and he was resigned to it. For more than an hour, while Luvie filled and refilled their cups with tea, Red and Otey and Stone Bull talked and Edith translated. She spoke Cheyenne well, and several times Stone Bull watched her translate and his stern lips almost smiled.

It was easy for Red to see that the old chief, whose black braids were just beginning to streak with gray, was fond of her. They talked slowly, Red pacing the conversation to the pitch of Indian talk, of cattle and hunting and horses and finally of whisky, which Stone Bull said was going to kill his people.

It was the time and the place then for Red to bring up his business. Red said to Edith, "Tell him it is not the fault of his people, but of ours. The fault of one man."

Stone Bull nodded gravely at that, and Red went on to enumerate the sins of Corb. Among them was his persecution of Frank, the friend of Morg Wheelon, who had been Stone Bull's friend. Today Corb had betrayed the Indian people and the whites by setting bad Indians on the trail herd. And now it seemed as if all the Indians and all the whites would fight. Stone Bull said the old ones wouldn't but the young ones wanted to. They were dancing tonight. Perhaps in two or three days, when their blood was hot with the throb of the drums, they would fight. Perhaps not.

"Ask him if he wants that," Red said.

Stone Bull said he didn't.

"Ask him if he wants to stop it." Stone Bull said he did.

Red leaned forward excitedly and looked at Stone Bull while he talked to Edith. "Tell him careful, Edith." And he began to really talk.

At midnight Frank was wakened by the rattle of a heavy key in the lock of his cell. Then the door opened and he was blinded by the light of a lantern.

"Roll out, Christian," a quiet voice said. "We're ridin'."

"Where?"

"Kansas."

Frank bent down to get his boots and swung his feet to the floor. So they were taking him to Kansas. He wondered what additional crimes he was charged with, for this afternoon he had heard his guards gossiping about the coming Indian trouble. Whatever it was, he could not expect leniency from the government, who had first put a reward for him as an escaped whisky peddler, later as a murderer, and now could add the crimes of violence against an officer, horse stealing and inciting the Indians to rebellion, not to mention complicity in the death of seven government wards, the Cheyennes. It was a nice list, he thought grimly.

He was prodded out the door by the officer and saw a dozen uniformed troopers standing in loose formation.

The officer said to the sentry, "Remember, you're to lock this door and carry on exactly as if you had a prisoner inside. No Indians allowed closer than fifty paces, and no callers. Have you got that?"

"Yes sir."

The lantern was extinguished, and with only a beam of light from a small bull's-eye lantern Frank was led to the horses. He was mounted, and they rode out of the post, past the dark stables, onto the prairie. Unless a man knew of it, their departure was unobtrusive and secret. Once clear of the garrison buildings they halted, and a halter rope was tied to the bridle of Frank's horse.

The captain in charge rode up beside him and said, "You make one break, Christian, and you're dead. We'll save the courts the cost of hanging you."

Frank didn't say anything, and the officer gave the command to move. It was a quiet ride and a fast one. They kept clear of any used trails and headed north. Once or twice the Cheyenne half-breed scout spoke to the officer, who changed directions, but there was little talk.

Frank thought it must be close to dawn when the officer called a halt, struck a match and looked at his watch.

"Find a camping spot in half an hour," he told the scout. "I want plenty of shelter. I'm allowing enough time so we'll be fed and hidden by daylight."

The scout grunted assent and presently changed his course and brought the detail into a stand of timber. He seemed to know his way, for he called a halt, and Frank heard the scout's horse drinking.

"Dismount," the officer called. "Remember, no fire. Break out your rations, eat and then turn in. Reilly, you and Morehouse are on the first watch." He was coming closer as he talked. He stopped and ordered Frank to dismount. Frank did, and then he was handcuffed and leg-ironed and his horse was taken away. His blankets were spread on the ground and he sat down, and presently someone loomed up before him and gave him dry rations and a canteen to drink from. Over beyond the water someone was making the picket line, and presently he heard the horses champing their corn. It was a strange camp, and Frank wondered at the precautions. When he was finished eating the sentries were posted and the blankets spread out. The troopers, usually friendly to everyone including prisoners, did not talk to him unless they had to, and then with bare civility. He had one on either side of him, and one of the sentries was posted at his head. The camp quieted, and Frank guessed that this trip would be a series of night marches, with layovers in the daytime, until they got to Kansas.

Slowly the camp went to sleep, and he could hear the even breathing of the troopers. Dawn was still not here, and he was not sleepy. Presently he heard the sentry behind him move. Then the muffled flare of a match bloomed and was quickly hidden, and he smelt the rank smoke of a sour pipe.

The sentry leaned over him and said, "A word out of you about this smoke, and ye'll rue it, me lad."

Frank didn't reply. He was beating his brain for some plan

of escape, but this was foolproof. He made a movement, and his stiff ground sheet telegraphed it to the sentry, who stirred and murmured, "Quiet."

Then silence again. Off across the camp there was a slight stirring. Frank listened to it die out. That must have been the other sentry, he thought.

Then, from behind him, there was a whisper of movement. The ground trembled a little and a leaf rustled, and then the sentry's pipe fell beside his head. Frank looked up and could see nothing. There was no sound. Maybe the man had gone to sleep.

Off across the way there was a stirring among the horses. It was low and steady, and he heard the soft hoof falls faintly. There was an uneasiness over there and it lasted about fifteen minutes, after which there was a strange and complete silence. Frank listened until the blood beat in his ears, and suddenly it came to him. The horses had moved!

He lay there, his heart hammering. What was going on here? Abruptly he caught a whiff of strange odor, the odor of smoked hide. It was faint and then it vanished, and again there was a trembling of the ground. But he could see nothing and heard only the slow breathing of the sleeping troopers on either side of him.

He was lying there with his eyes open, listening, when a hand settled over his mouth. His instinct was to cry out, and as his throat tightened the hand firmed on his lips. But when he relaxed it lessened and presently drew away. Then he felt something fumbling with his leg irons. Ever so gently they were unlocked and removed. Now he could smell smoked hide plainly. Then the hands came to his wrists and his handcuffs were unlocked. Gently his feet were lifted off the noisy ground sheet and placed carefully on the ground. Then hands caught both of his and he was silently hauled to his feet and steadied. His hand was taken and he was led into the trees, and the only sound he heard was the sound he himself was making in walking. He might have been led by a ghost, it was so quiet.

He knew then that this was neither Red nor Otey, but an Indian. When he had been taken deep into the timber the man leading him stopped. Suddenly the bull's-eye lantern flashed on, and before him he saw the captain, his neckerchief gagging his mouth, tied to a tree. At his feet were the two bound and gagged sentries. Tied beside him was the scout, ungagged, but a painted spear, with a horsetail plume at the juncture of shaft and head, was placed against his breast, its haft vanishing behind the light.

Frank's leader stopped him gently, and then there was guttural speech in Cheyenne from behind the light.

The scout, whose forehead was beaded with sweat, grunted and turned his head and said to the captain, "They say they take the white prisoner out to kill him. It is payment for the death of their seven brothers."

Frank's spine stiffened. He could see the head of the Indian ahead of him black against the circle of light on the two captives. The Indian turned, shook his head in negation, and his hand caught Frank's in a silent handshake. As plainly as it could be told without words, this meant that Frank was their friend and that he was not to believe what the spokesman was saying. Frank held his breath, listening.

The Indian behind the light spoke again, and the scout translated again to the captain: "They say they will kill us someday, but not now." And the scout added bitterly, in the same tone of voice, "It's that wild bunch of bucks that Corb runs."

At mention of Corb's name the spear moved and the scout flinched. Then suddenly the light went out, there was a whisper of activity, and Frank was led by the hand out of the stand of timber.

Once outside the trees, he could see the east beginning to gray. Against it he counted the heads of seventeen Indians.

He spoke then in Comanche. "Who are my friends?"

One man answered, "Stone Bull's friends."

The reins of a horse were put in his hands, and the Indians moved off. Presently he was alone. And as fast as his horse could take him Frank rode away from the timber.

Chapter XVII

CORB COULD READ Indian signs as well as any man in the Nations. When news was brought to him at his place that Frank Christian had been captured, but only after he and his crew had killed seven Cheyennes, Corb's face showed no elation. The good news was more than canceled by the bad. He had miscalculated on several things. He hadn't counted on Christian throwing in with Barnes and, above all, he hadn't counted on Barnes fighting the Indians. The big fat fool, probably egged on by that wild Red Shibe and Christian, had lost his head, and it looked as if the fat was in the fire. And Corb didn't like Indian trouble. It scared him.

He declined to join the card game that night and waited impatiently for his riders to drift in from Reno with their reports. And each man returning from Reno had a story of increasing gravity. The Indians had deserted the post and the agency, and trouble was brewing in their camp. Long after his riders had turned in, Corb sat up waiting for the last of his men, Beach Freeman. Well after midnight he heard Beach's horse cross the corral lot to the horse pasture. Beach was singing drunk, and Corb, playing a nervous game of solitaire on the big table, listened to it and his eyes narrowed.

When Beach came into the house, tramped through the back rooms and stuck his head in the front room to see who was up Corb was smoking a thin cigar, his chair backtilted against the wall and his hands idle.

"Howdy, boss," Beach said and grinned.

"Come in," Corb said.

Beach was already swaggering into the room. He threw his hat down on the table and sank into a chair. Corb eyed him with cold distaste.

Beach said, "Looks like they're goin' to nail Frank's hide up for sure."

Corb didn't say anything.

"They're takin' him to Kansas tomorrow morning."

Corb said, "What about the Indians?"

Beach grinned. "They're dancin' tonight. You can hear the drums at the post. Everybody's driftin' into the garrison. The whole damn country's scared."

"And you're not," Corb said dryly.

"Of what?" Beach sneered. "Them black devils has only got bows and arrows and spears."

Corb didn't bother to tell him that he himself had picked up a little money by running guns to the Indians until he saw that his shortsighted policy might result in getting himself shot, along with all the other whites. Corb got up, walked around the table and paused in front of Beach.

"Kid, you drink too much," Corb said. "Better quit it."

But drunken talk or not, Corb knew truth when he heard it, and Beach's information gave him an uneasy night. By next noon Corb could stand it no longer. He dressed in a fresh black suit and clean shirt and announced to his crew that he was riding into Reno until this Indian scare was over. He'd advise them to do the same. Turn the horses loose and leave the place. And any man caught selling liquor to an Indian had better take the money and get out of the country before he found it out. He ordered the buckboard hitched and drove off toward Reno without another word. Beach Freeman was the first to saddle up and catch up with him. Three others followed, and the rest decided to come later.

The garrison, as Beach had informed him last night, was filling up. All the agency folk from Darlington had moved over to the hotel during the morning, and Corb was hard put to get a room. The saloon was thronged, and off on the flats behind the wagon yard a cluster of tents was going up. The garrison was policed and guarded this morning by sentries, and there was a tension in the air in spite of the holiday spirit.

Corb greeted a few friends, then headed for the barbershop, and Beach, who had seen tagging him around, ducked into the sutler's bar as soon as Corb was gone.

Corb had a long wait for a chair but finally took his turn. His lank pale hair was cut, and then the barber stretched him out for a shave.

He was lathering Corb's face, listening idly to the leisurely chatter of the customers, when an army orderly came in the door.

"Corb here?" he asked.

Corb twisted his head and answered, "Here."

"Major's compliments, Mr Corb. He wants to see you."

"Now?"

"I reckon so, sir."

Corb's face was wiped clean of lather; he rose, put on his loose black tie and went out with the orderly. They crossed the parade ground, and Corb was ushered into the administration office. In the largest corner room Major Corning was pacing the floor in front of his big desk, behind which were the American and several regimental colors. A burly captain looking a little the worse for wear was seated in a chair, but at Corb's entrance he rose too.

The major dismissed the orderly, then said to Corb, "This is Captain McEachern, Corb."

They didn't shake hands, and Corb only got the briefest nod from the captain.

"Sit down," Major Corning invited brusquely.

Corb took a chair, and Major Corning sat on the desk. He had a studious face and thin sandy hair, but right now his jaw was set and his pale eyes altogether unpleasant.

"Corb," he said, "this is once you've gone a little too far. That affair last night cinched it."

Corb's frown was cautious. He observed the captain glaring at him, and a blind man could see that Major Corning was angry.

"You've got the best of me," Corb said. "I don't know what you're talking about."

Major Corning's face took on some color. "I expected that," he snapped. "Captain, tell your story. Then we'll get down to business."

Captain McEachern told in detail of how his camp had been raided by Indians last night. They had tied him and his sentries and his scout and had taken Frank Christian away from them. They left with the promise that they would kill Christian for his slaughter of the seven bucks during the fight with the trail herders. "When the camp roused at daylight and found me and the horses Christian was gone," he finished.

Corb didn't speak for a moment, and then he said dryly, "And you think I sent them?"

Major Corning said, "It was you and Milabel who induced the agent to put a price on Christian's head. It was you who tried to corner him at Barnes's place. I don't concern myself much with the rows between you cattlemen, but I do know you and Christian have been feuding ever since he came here. And those Indians mentioned your name."

Corb said gently, his face cautious, his eyes wary, "It couldn't be done. Not by me."

Major Corning leaned toward Corb, and his mouth was grim. "Let's be frank, Corb. Or I will. I know you peddle whisky here on the reservation. You peddle it to the Indians, against the law. I've tried more than once to get evidence against you, but I can't do it. Still, I know you're guilty. I also know that you have influence with a certain faction of the Cheyennes and that you claim to be their lease agent for these reservation lands." He paused to glare at Corb. "When you tell me you haven't enough influence with these Indians to pull off something like last night I say you're a liar!"

Corb's eyes flickered with anger, but his face didn't change. He leaned back in his chair, drew out a cigar, lighted it and threw the match on the floor.

"I'm not admitting anything," he murmured. "But supposing what you say is true, what do you propose to do?"

"Arrest you."

"On what grounds?"

"Seizing a prisoner from United States soldiers and killing him."

Corb smiled under his roan mustache. "I'm no lawyer, Major, but I know if you're going to prove murder you've got to have a body. Have you got one?"

Major Corning said, "No," reluctantly.

"Witnesses?"

"My interpreter," Captain McEachern said.

"Did he see me?"

"No. But he heard your Indians mention you."

"Anybody can mention my name," Corb said thinly. "If someone wanted to throw the blame on me he'd be mighty sure to mention my name." He spread his hands. "You haven't got a body, you haven't got a witness, and I'll bet money you haven't questioned a single Indian."

"We can't, dammit!" the major exploded. "We don't know who they are."

Corb smiled. "Your case won't hold water, Major."

"Then I'll get you for setting those bucks to raiding Hopewell Barnes's trail herd!"

"I don't think you will," Corb said. "You know and I know that the agency beef ration isn't half enough to feed these Indians. You've winked at their raiding passing herds for years. Punch them this time and you'll have an insurrection of starving Indians."

Major Corning came off the desk and started to pace the room, glaring at Corb. And Corb, for his part, was smiling, regarding his cigar and rolling it between his fingers.

"The trouble with all this, Major, is that you're bluffing," he said. "You went about it wrong. If you had anything on me you wouldn't be arguing. And if you go through with my arrest and try me with no evidence you'll get a reprimand." He glanced evenly at the major, who was eying him in wrath. "And every major wants to be a colonel, doesn't he?"

Corb had the whip hand and he knew it, and he was a man who had got ahead by pressing his advantage. He leaned forward and said evenly, "Do you still say I'm under arrest, Major?"

Captain McEachern and Major Corning looked at each

other, and Corb could tell what they were thinking. Time and again they had tried to get evidence of his whisky running and herd raiding and had failed. That left only the seizure of Frank Christian. And McEachern's report in court would be humiliating to the service and would bring a reprimand on the major. They were, in other words, not willing to take the risk.

Corb rose. "I take it I'm not."

"One last thing, Corb," Major Corning said in a voice trembling with anger. "I'm commandant of this post. In an emergency I have emergency orders. And in order to hold you here until we get evidence, I'm putting every white on this reservation under protective arrest and confining them to the military reservation. That means you."

Corb laughed gently. "You couldn't drive me off, Major. Good day." And he sauntered back to the barbershop in the late afternoon sun. He wished he knew what had happened to Christian, though.

After Stone Bull had left the Barnes place all of them decided that it was no longer safe for Edith to stay alone nights at her place, and Luvie had her stay the night.

Next morning, when Luvie wakened, Edith was gone. So was Red. There wasn't so much as a note to indicate why they had left or for where. Luvie roused Otey and her father, and after a look in the stable Otey came with the information that their horses were gone too.

"But where?" Luvie asked. "They can't go anywhere during this Indian scare!"

A week ago Otey would have bitterly denounced Red for running out on them, but now he held his tongue.

"If Edith's with Red she's safe," Otey said. "It ain't important. What we got to do is go over to the post and see what's happenin'."

"All of us," Barnes said firmly. "If the Indians break out they'll come here first. And I don't intend to have Luvie here. Last night, at Major Corning's insistence, I engaged rooms in the hotel for the lot of us. Now move, Luvie, and get us some breakfast. We're leaving the place right away."

But after a hurried breakfast Otey leaned back in his chair and stated that he was not leaving. If Stone Bull's ruse worked and Frank was free, he would come here first. If he didn't find anyone, where could he go? Otey was adamant in the face of Luvie's and Barnes's arguments, so they left him and joined the stream of Darlington townspeople who were moving over to the protection of the garrison.

The post was thronged, but Luvie, following Otey's advice, secured a chair on the porch in front of the post store and settled down to a day of waiting and watching. Around noon she was rewarded by seeing Captain McEachern's crestfallen detail return to the post empty handed, and for the first time in twenty-four hours she breathed easily again. She started out to find her father, but in ten steps she saw him leaning against a porch post talking to a group of men. When he saw her he nodded his head and winked solemnly at her, and she knew he had seen too.

She forgot about eating and took up her vigil again. One part of Red's plan had worked; would the other part work too?

In early afternoon she saw Scott Corb, dressed in a neat black suit and shined boots, climb the porch steps. At his heels was a fresh-faced and arrogant young man wearing shiny new boots and a new dust-colored Stetson. The expression on his face made Luvie want to laugh. He looked as if he were inordinately proud of his new outfit and at the same time as if his boots were so new that they hurt him to walk. But what was most incongruous of all was that he should be with Corb. There were others with Corb, still-faced, hard-eyed and dirty men, and this raw young man looked like a sheep among wolves.

Barnes had seen Corb come too, and now he sagged into a chair beside Luvie. They knew what to look for and kept their attention on the doors of the administration building across the parade ground. It was a matter of only a few minutes before an orderly left the administration offices and walked purposefully toward the hotel, threading through the crowd. He went into the barbershop and in a minute came out again. Scott Corb was with him, and they went directly to the administration building.

Barnes looked at Luvie, a grim smile on his face. "It looks like business," he grunted. "Now you get something to eat."

"But I want to wait and see what happens to him!" Luvie said.

"Go get something to eat at the restaurant. I'll watch. Now run along."

It took Luvie an impatient half-hour to get a place in the crowded restaurant. Even when she was served she found that her excitement had evaporated her hunger, but she struggled bravely with unwanted food.

When she finally finished and returned to her father she took one look at his crestfallen face and said, "Dad, what happened?"

"Corb's free," Barnes said gloomily. He looked up at her, his face puzzled. "Somethin' went wrong, Luvie. He walked out of there alone and went into the barbershop whistlin'."

Luvie sank into a chair, staring at him. "And Frank?"

"He must be loose," Barnes reasoned. "How come the detail came in empty handed? And how come Corb was called to the major's office?" He shook his head and sighed. "He's just too damn big to knock over, girl. That's all." He looked obliquely at her. "If you was a boy instead of a girl, I'd ask you to come along with me."

"Where?"

"To the bar. I'm goin' to try and get the taste of that out of my mouth." He got up and left.

Luvie settled back in her chair to await darkness and word from Otey, struggling against the disappointment she felt. If Corb had been arrested and held by the army, then there would have been some chance for Frank. He could return and clear his name of all these fantastic charges. But now it seemed hopeless. What was to stop Frank from talking with Otey and deciding that this country was too hot for him and heading back for Texas? What was keeping him here? Nothing, now.

She started conversation with an agency woman beside her so she wouldn't think of these things. In a few moments the word passed through the crowd that all persons were forbidden to leave the military reservations. It was confirmed when the guard was doubled on all four sides of the grounds. Rumor had it that the Indians were certain to attack now and that the garrison was really in a state of siege. Orders were posted on the post-office bulletin board that one mess hall was being set aside for civilian use, and this bore out the rumor. Out on the parade grounds, where it was relatively quiet, it was easy to hear the sound of the distant Indian drums, and opinion was that the Cheyennes were now inducing the more peaceful Arapahos to join the coming insurrection.

Just before dark a scouting detail rode up the slope from Darlington, herding a handful of whites who had elected to risk the Indian attack. Their orders had been to round up all the whites in Darlington and force them to accept army protection. And among those whites was Otey, his face angry and his jaw set.

Luvie ran out toward the stables and met him coming out.

"What about Frank?" she asked.

"Didn't come," Otey growled. "Probably waitin' until dark. And them damn yellowlegs wouldn't let me stay at the house." He glared at her. "Whose neck am I riskin', anyhow?"

"They won't let anybody go out of the garrison grounds either," Luvie said.

"They'll play hell keepin' me here," Otey said. "Wait till it gets dark. I'm goin' to meet Frank, and the whole army can't stop me!"

Barnes called them all to supper then, and while Otey ate Luvie told him of what had happened today. It was almost certain that Frank was free. But Corb hadn't been held by the army. He was here at the post now, confined like all the others by the army edict.

Otey said little, and when he finished eating he excused himself and left. Luvie, half sick with worry and sunk in the deepest gloom, went up to her room and lay down on the bed, staring at the ceiling. If only she could turn back the calendar to that afternoon when Corb induced her to betray Frank. All this was her fault, and she had only herself to thank. But what hurt most, what she would never forget, was the quiet steady way Frank Christian had told her that he never wanted to see her again. There was no use fooling herself; she hadn't been woman enough to recognize a real man when she saw him, and now she had lost him.

She was roused from her thoughts by a knock on the door, and Otey stepped in. Without a word he crossed over to a chair and sat down.

"No luck, Otey?"

"They got all the horse corrals guarded and wouldn't give me my horse. When I tried to break through the line of sentries I got throwed back twice."

Luvie didn't say anything. If Frank returned to the house tonight he would think they all had forsaken him. Why wouldn't he ride out for Texas? Luvie looked over at Otey, at his bitter face and his expression of wounded pride. She laughed ruefully, and Otey grinned faintly.

Barnes came in then. His face was purple with anger, and he slammed his hat down on the bed. When he caught sight of Otey he said, "Otey, give me your gun."

"What for?" Otey asked.

"Corb has got a rider down there that I'm goin' to fill so full of lead he couldn't float on hard butter."

Luvie came over to him. "Why, Dad! I've never seen you this way. What is it?"

"I've taken enough rawhidin'! He's a fresh kid and drunk. He started rawhidin' me about killin' those Indians. Said if it wasn't for us and for Frank there wouldn't be an Indian scare. Corb shut him up, but he's still talkin' pretty wide about Frank."

Luvie nodded. "I saw him. But he's only a boy. You couldn't fight him."

Otey's attention sharpened. "What did he look like?"

"He's got a face that makes you itch to slug it. Young, thin, light hair, green eyes, spoiled mouth."

Otey came slowly to his feet. "You hear anybody name him?"

"Corb called him Beach."

"Ah," Otey said. He started for the door.

Barnes said. "Where you goin'?"

"To pay a call," Otey said. "You stay here."

He went downstairs to the porch and walked along it till he came to the big window of the sutler's bar. The place was thronged, but, looking through the window, he could see Corb and four of his men at the corner table playing poker. And at the bar, back turned to it and elbows on it, watching the game, was Beach Freeman, a glass in his hand. So Beach hadn't gone back to Texas, Otey thought sourly. And he knew he had the answer to something that had been troubling him a long time. How had Corb known that a note from Luvie would toll Frank into Barnes's place for that bushwhack, unless somebody had told him? That somebody was Beach, who had heard enough and seen enough around the chuck wagon to put two and two together. Otey felt a hot wrath crawling inside him, but it wasn't so hot that he lost his head.

He slipped back into the darkness, walked down the long porch, through the gate into the wagon compound, where a lantern was hanging over the feed-office door, and into the stable. He took the stable lantern off its nail and climbed into the hayloft. There, as was almost always the case in any public stable loft, were a half-dozen men asleep. They were the riffraff, the drunks and the men down on their luck.

Otey looked them over, and when he came to one bleary and unshaven sleeper he stirred him with his toe. The man roused, and Otey said, "You want to earn five dollars?"

"Sure."

"Come along."

Outside the stable door Otey smelled the sour smell of long-drunk whisky on the man's breath, and he knew he had chosen wisely. He gave the man a five-dollar gold piece, and the man looked at it and said, "What do I do?"

"Go in the sutler's bar and drink it up," Otey said. "First, though, do you know Beach Freeman?"

"No."

"Ask the bartender. He'll point him out. Tell Beach that the hostler says that if he don't pay his feed bill tonight he's goin' to turn his horse loose. You got it?"

The man repeated it after him and then left in a hurry for the bar. Otey knew that Beach didn't owe a feed bill. But the threat of having his horse turned loose, even if by mistake, would bring him out. And the messenger, with drinking money in his fist, couldn't be pried away from the bar.

Otey drifted over to the shadow of the wagon shed and waited. It was five minutes before he heard a man swing into the compound gate. Beach swaggered into the circle of lantern light, his face belligerent, his eyes on the feed-office door.

From the corner of the office Otey drawled, "Hello, Beach."

Beach hauled up and stared into the darkness. When Otey stepped into the light, his gun leveled at Beach, there was a moment of utter silence. Beach licked his lips, and slowly his hands raised over his head.

"Step over, Beach," Otey drawled. "I never liked your face, and I reckon it's about time I made it over."

And Beach came, his mouth dry and his throat tight, into the darkness.

Chapter XVIII

MILABEL TOOK HIS SIESTA on the couch in his office every afternoon during hot weather. It was a custom he had picked up from the pelados in south Texas and one which nothing short of a trail drive could interrupt, not even an Indian scare. His crew, full strength, had elected to wait out the Indian scare at the ranch, confident of their numbers, and Milabel had sided with them. Even in case of trouble he favored taking a chance and saving the company property. This afternoon he lay at full length on the couch, a Stockman's Gazette over his face to shut out the sunlight. He was just on the drowsy borderland of sleep when he felt the couch sag abruptly. It took some seconds for his sleepy brain to telegraph the news to his hands that someone just sat down on the couch near his feet.

He opened his eyes, raised his hands to the Gazette, lifted it and saw Frank Christian sitting by his knees. What yanked him awake was the black barrel of the Colt .45 which he was looking into.

Milabel frowned. "You again. I thought you was in jail." There was not fear in his voice, only disgust and amazement.

Frank didn't smile. In fact, his face looked as if he never intended to smile again. His checks were haggard, and his eyes were deep sunk, sultry, the color of roiled smoke. There was a grimness in his unsmiling mouth, an alertness in his movements and manner that told Milabel he was looking at trouble.

Frank tossed something on Milabel's chest and said, "That yours?" watching him carefully.

Milabel leisurely picked up the object and looked at it. It was a silver spur rowel as large as a dollar, with wickedly sharp points and some fine hammered-work design. The fork and part of the shank were attached to the rowel, but just beyond the fork the shank had been broken off. Milabel looked up and said, "No. It ain't mine."

Frank stood up and said, "Get on your feet!"

His voice had iron in it, and Milabel obeyed with alacrity. "Turn around."

Milabel did, and Frank knelt to look at his spurs. They were plain, with a gooseneck shank and small blunt rowel.

"Got any other spurs?" Frank asked.

Milabel turned around. "No."

"Where do you sleep?"

Milabel nodded toward the door into an adjoining room. "Why?"

"Get in there and pull all your stuff out and throw it on the floor. Go on."

Frank prodded him into the bedroom. Angrily Milabel dumped the contents of drawers in a pile on the floor. Then his clothes followed, until every single thing he owned lay stacked in the middle of the floor. His broad face was beet red when he had finished. Frank said, "That all?"

"Listen, Christian. I ain't got but one pair of spurs. What in hell are you after?"

"You don't know?"

"I don't know nothin'!" Milabel said angrily. "I don't know how you got past my guards! Now that you're here I don't know what you're after!"

Frank looked at him steadily. "I'm after Morg Wheelon's killer, Milabel. That spur rowel was lost the night Morg was gunned. The man who lost it killed Morg, and he's still wearin' the patched spur."

Milabel's broad face was grim looking. He looked steadily at Frank and said, "You know that for sure?"

"I got it from a man who saw the fight."

Milabel nodded. "And you're here to see if I'm wearin' the patched spur, or any of my men, eh?"

"That's right."

Milabel said harshly, "Christian, you and me have tangled plenty, and we'll tangle again, I reckon. But you ain't learned yet that even if I run a tough outfit here I run a straight one. You found us in Wheelon's place because we wanted his range and we moved onto it after he was killed. But that's a hell of a lot different than killin' a man in cold blood. I wouldn't kill a man like that and I'd see any man in my crew hung that did it. And I'm goin' to prove it to you."

"You sure are," Frank said softly.

"You can carry that gun or throw it away," Milabel said. "It don't make no difference. You're goin' to see everything this outfit owns!"

He strode past Frank and into the office. His shell belt and gun were lying under his hat. He picked up his Stetson,

paying no attention to the gun, and tramped out the door.
Frank followed him over to the long bunkhouse where a
couple of men were lounging in the door.

Frank tried to conceal his gun behind Milabel, but thirty
yards from the bunkhouse he saw one of the men dodge back
into the room, and he knew he was recognized.

Milabel raised his voice. "Barney, put down that gun! That
goes for all of you. Jess, roust out the whole crew. The first
man that shoots will get shot himself, and that's a promise.
Step outside here and line up!"

Slowly the surly crew filed out facing Milabel. They were
watching Frank, who had holstered his gun when he heard
Milabel's orders. When the crew, twenty-six in all, were
formed in a loose half circle around Milabel he said, "Christian here wants to look at your spurs. Stand where you are
and keep quiet."

Frank walked back of the men and went down the line
examining each pair of spurs. Some of the men were in sock
feet and some were not wearing spurs on their boots. No set
of spurs, either in size or in the elaboration of the silverwork,
resembled the rowel he had in his pocket.

When he was through Milabel said, "All right, Christian.
Step in the bunkhouse and keep an eye on the men. Now
you boys go back and dump out your war bags in front of
your bunks."

They went back and dumped their war bags, and Frank
went down the line. There were extra sets of spurs in some
of the war bags, and once Frank knelt by one rider's boots
to compare the rowels, but they were not the same.

Finished, Milabel said, "Anywhere else you want to look?
Blacksmith shop, wagon shed, any of the buildings?"

"All of them," Frank said quietly.

Patiently Milabel let him poke anywhere he pleased.
He found some discarded and worn-out spurs in the blacksmith shop but still nothing that resembled his rowel. Gus
had said the man was still wearing them. Nobody here was
wearing the mate, that was certain.

When he was finished he nodded to Milabel. "Thanks. As
soon as I take a look at the guard I slipped past I'll be
satisfied."

Milabel called for a horse and rode out with Frank to the
rise behind the house where the guard was sitting by his
horse. His spurs didn't match either.

Frank swung onto his horse again, and Milabel said, "I am

curious, Christian. It ain't any of my business, but do you aim to hog-tie every man in the Nations to find out if he's got the mate to that rowel?"

"If I have to."

"Word'll get around, and whoever has it will throw it away. Not to mention the fact that the whole damn army will be chasin' you in another day."

"There's just two outfits that can own it, Milabel," Frank said curtly. "You are one."

"Who's the other?"

Frank said thinly, "Never mind."

"It's Corb's, isn't it?"

Frank didn't say anything.

Milabel swng into the saddle. "There's one sure way to pull you off my neck," Milabel said. "That's to help you locate that spur. I'll ride to Corb's with you."

"And throw in with his crew when we get there?" Frank asked dryly. "No, thanks."

"You got two guns, I got none," Milabel pointed out. "I may be able to save you some trouble with Corb."

Frank hesitated a long time, pondering his chances. If Corb's crew was there they wouldn't be as docile as the Circle R crew. They'd fight. Now Corb and Milabel were partners of a sort, and it might be that Milabel could talk Corb into letting Frank look. It wouldn't hurt to try.

"All right," he said.

They arrived at Corb's place at dust. The house seemed deserted, and Frank cautiously approached the place. They dismounted, and he made Milabel keep between him and the house. Achieving the front door, which was open, they entered and heard the soft snoring of a sleeping man. Frank looked into the front room and saw a man sleeping at the table, his head lying on his folded arms, an overturned bottle of whisky beside him. There was no other sound in the house.

Frank cursed softly, again remembering what Gus had said. Whoever owned the mended spur was wearing it. And Corb's crew was gone. He went over to the sleeping man and knelt beside him. The puncher was not wearing spurs. Frank looked up at Milabel.

"Tough luck," Milabel said. "You aim to wait till they ride in?"

"That's right. I'll look their stuff over now."

Frank went upstairs and turned into the first room he came to, the corner room. It held an old iron bed on which was a tangle of dirty blankets. Clothes were strewn over the floor, and on the deerskin rug was a pair of pants. Frank moved them aside with his toe, and under them was a pair of boots. On the floor beside them were spurs.

Frank knelt and picked one up. As he examined the rowel his heart almost missed a beat. The stamping on the big rowel was like the one in his pocket. With trembling fingers he rose and lighted the lamp and set it on the floor. He compared the two rowels carefully. They were identical.

He dropped the one spur and picked up its mate. The rowel on the mate was different!

He turned the spur over and examined the shank. And there, behind the fork, was the welded place where the plain rowel and shank had been joined!

He took the stairs two at a time, ran past Milabel in the hall and into the room where the puncher was sleeping. He kicked the man's chair out from under him, yanked him to his feet and slapped his face viciously. The man roused and tried to shield his face with his arms, and Frank slapped him again. Then he shoved the man to the door, into the hall, and kicked him up the stairs. The puncher, still three-quarters drunk, yelled and cursed and fought. Frank kicked him onto the landing, then picked him up by the scruff of his neck and dragged him into the room and stood him on his feet.

He shoved the pair of spurs in front of his eyes and said, "Who owns these?"

Slowly the puncher's eyes focused. "Them spurs?" he asked thickly.

"Yes."

"Where'd you find 'em?" the puncher asked.

"Here. In this room."

"Must be Corb's," the puncher muttered. "He sleeps here."

"Where is he?"

"Reno."

Frank shoved the puncher toward the bed, ran past Milabel, who had come upstairs to watch, and took the stairs in two leaps. And Milabel, excitement in his eyes, was close on his heels.

Luvie had scarcely succeeded in calming her father down after Otey left before there was a loud knock on her room door. She opened to find Edith standing there.

"Luvie, where's your dad?"

"Here," Luvie said. "Where have you——"

Edith brushed past her and ran over to Barnes. "Come with me, Mr Barnes. We've got to see the colonel, and the soldiers won't let us. They're trying to keep Red off the grounds."

"But what's happened?"

"Get Major Corning and bring him out to the Darlington road!" Edith said excitedly. "He'll come for you! Please hurry."

Barnes, bewildered, nevertheless obeyed. He and Edith and Luvie hurried across the parade grounds to the administration building, where the lights were still burning. A sentry posted at the door of Major Corning's office tried to stop them, but Barnes shoved him aside and threw open the door. Major Corning was talking to an officer, and he reared up at sight of them.

Edith brushed past Barnes and hurried to his desk. "Major Corning, come with me at once, please!"

"But why—where—"

"If you want to stop this Indian trouble come with me!"

Major Corning walked from behind his desk and followed Edith out of the room and outside, Luvie and Barnes trailing her. Edith led them around the building and out on the Darlington road. At the edge of the buildings there were two sentries, a lantern between them, standing in the middle of the road. Their rifles were leveled at Red, who stood with his hands on his hips holding the reins of two horses, his own and Edith's.

Major Corning slowed up at sight of him, exasperation showing in his face. He said, "Now what's this?"

"Listen careful," Red said in a low, angry voice. "I ain't goin' to say it twice. Stone Bull, the old Cheyenne chief, has had the ringleaders of this uprisin' in his lodge since noon. He's been servin' 'em Scott Corb's trade whisky that I stole out of a cache. Edith Fairing and me have been talkin' to them alongside of Stone Bull all afternoon, tryin' to get 'em to change their minds. They were fightin' mad when the whisky began to work, but they're all right now." He paused.

"They're hog drunk and sleepin'. If you send a detail of soldiers with an ambulance to Stone Bull's lodge, you can freight the whole bunch of 'em over to the guardhouse here, and your rebellion's over."

"Over?" Corning asked, his voice skeptical. "Do you think the arrest of a few will help us any?"

"Let me finish," Red said. "Stone Bull says if you send your wisest officer into camp with some soldiers to back him up and tell the Cheyennes and Arapahos that the government is increasing their beef ration and that you're holdin' a special beef issue tomorrow, there won't be any revolt. Them Indians are starvin', Major! Arrest the leaders and feed the rest, and your trouble is over!"

Major Corning was silent a long moment, staring at Red in the lantern light. "If I thought I could believe you I'd—"

"Don't believe me!" Red yelled angrily. "Believe her!" He pointed to Edith. "She's been sittin' in a lodge all day while them drunken Cheyennes threatened her with scalpin' and torture and everything else! She's the one to believe! Ask her!"

Major Corning wheeled to face Edith.

"Do it, Major Corning!" Edith said. "Believe me, I know those people! I know that Stone Bull and the others want peace and that once the ringleaders—Corb's Indians—are arrested the trouble will be over. Arrest those leaders, promise the others food and keep your word! The uprising will be over then!"

Major Corning stared at her tense, beautiful face and then, forgetting all dignity, he wheeled and yelled to the officer watching them from a window of the administration building: "Brett, have assembly sounded! No, wait a minute!" And he turned and ran, major or no major.

And even as he was running there came the sound of gunfire from the sutler's bar.

Chapter XIX

THEY WERE IN SIGHT of the sentries, soon to be challenged, when Milabel said again to Frank, "Sure you want to do this, Christian? You've got a price on your head, you've escaped, you've—"

Frank said quietly, "Get me past the sentries. I'll worry about the rest of it."

Milabel grunted. They pulled up at the sentry's challenge, "Who goes there?"

"Chet Milabel, from the Circle R. This is one of my men."

"All right, Milabel. Leave your horse with the troopers at the corral."

They passed through the line and rode over to the corral behind the stable, where, in the darkness, they turned their horses over to a trooper who said, "You two didn't get in none too soon."

They walked through the long driveway of the stable and came out into the wagon yard. This, Frank remembered, was where he got his welcome to Fort Reno. That was from Corb too, he supposed.

Passing the office, they heard a scuffling back in the darkness of the wagon shed. Milabel glanced that way, but Frank stalked on. Suddenly someone yelled, "Frank!"

It was Otey's voice. Frank stopped and turned. Otey called, "Wait a minute!" There was a loud, sickening thud, the sound of thinly padded bone on flesh, followed by the sound of body hitting the ground. A moment later Otey walked out of the darkness. His nose was bloody and there was a cut over his eye and his knuckles were raw, but he seemed oblivious to that. He came up to Frank, looking around him, strapping on his gun belt.

"Great lord, get out of sight!"

Frank said, "Is Corb in the post?"

"You damn fool, there's two-three hundred men here with orders to kill you on sight!"

Frank wheeled and started walking toward the compound gate. Otey ran after him and grabbed him by the arm. "Frank, what is it?" he asked in a calm voice.

"Corb killed Morg, Otey. I found that spur, like Gus said. I found the mate to it and the mended one by Corb's bed out at his place."

Otey's hand came away from Frank's arm. "He's in the saloon, Frank. Just play it careful, and I'll back you."

Milabel, at the gate, said, "Here's where I drop out."

Otey said, "You better stay out too."

Frank said nothing. He mounted the porch and walked down the long length of it, his goal the saloon. At the window he hauled up and looked inside. The bar was less crowded now, but in the far corner, away from the window and in the angle made by the end of the bar, Corb still sat at his card game, his back to the wall, his face to the window.

Frank sized it up and knew he couldn't get ten feet past the doorsill before he was gunned. He said to Otey, "You cover 'em from the door, Otey."

He walked down to the end of the window, picked up a chair, raised it over his head and crashed it through the window in one great downraking sweep.

At the same time Otey lunged through the door and yelled: "Don't nobody move!"

And then Frank stepped through the hole in the window, a gun hanging in his hand, and the room fell silent.

Corb half raised out of his seat at sight of Frank, his eyes wild, then settled slowly back into his chair.

Frank said, "Corb, stand up!" And his voice cut the silence like a whip.

After a long pause Corb came to his feet beside the angle of the bar.

"Walk out of that corner and come out through the door onto the porch. And when you hit the porch cut loose your dogs, because I know you killed Morg."

Corb hesitated for one moment, took a step from behind the table, and when he was even with the bar he suddenly dived behind its shelter.

Frank swung up his gun and he saw he couldn't shoot for the drinkers lining the bar. He lunged through the crowd, flinging men aside, and swung into the space behind the bar just in time to see Corb duck into the door to the dark store beyond the other end of the bar.

He ran down behind the bar, knocking the bartender against the back bar, and dived into the dark door of the store beyond just as Otey let his gun off at the ceiling and yelled: "Everybody stay put!"

Corb's gun bellowed out, and a slug slapped into the door frame beside Frank. He moved over into the deep darkness of the store, and across the tables lined with goods he flipped two shots at Corb. He vaulted a table, saw a form move across the store again and shot once more. He had cut Corb off from retreating into the darker rear of the store. Now he had him between himself and the street lamps out on the parade grounds which glowed through the windows. Frank saw something move up ahead, and he shot again and heard the hammering of Corb's feet as he ran. Suddenly a bolt of dress goods soared toward the window, and it jangled outward onto the porch, and then Corb, half crouching, dived through the hole in the window.

He was running for the edge of the porch just as Red, attracted by the shot, came pounding across the parade grounds, saw him by the aid of the street lamp and flipped two shots at him. Frank threw two more through the window, and more glass jangled.

For a split second Corb hesitated, then he ran down the porch. Frank vaulted through the broken window in time to see him duck into the stairway that raised to the hotel rooms on the second floor.

Frank took after him and swung into the stair well. Up at the top Corb's form was just vanishing. Frank took the stairs three at a time, and Red swung in behind him, and Luvie, her skirts lifted, swung in behind Red.

Red yelled: "Careful comin' up the top, Frank!"

Frank hit the top step and tripped and sprawled just as Corb's gun cut loose from down the corridor. Frank threw a shot at him, and Corb ducked back into the L of the corridor, and Frank raced after him, listening to the distant pounding of Corb's feet.

Red hit the stair landing, pulling a gun, and wheeled just in time to jab it into Luvie. Red's mouth opened, then he grabbed her and pulled her out of sight just as the first of the barroom crowd, whom Otey could not hold any longer, hit the stair well below. Red shot down it twice and then heard the curses of the men below drifting up the stair well. One man shouted: "The back stairs! He can't guard both!"

Luvie heard and she said, "Quick, Red! Give me a gun!"

"But you're a woman! You can't——"

"I can fight for him, can't I?" Luvie flashed. "I tried to get him killed once! Oh, Red, give me a chance to make up for it!"

Red palmed up his second gun, gave it to Luvie and, with a sinking heart, watched her run down the corridor toward the back stairs, and his courage forsook him. Suppose something happened to her! He didn't have time to think of that long, for the second wave of pursuers—soldiers this time—hit the stairs. He laid a blistering fire down on them.

When Frank rounded the corner of the dark corridor he saw only a bracket wall lamp turned down low ahead of him. He lifted his gun and shot it out, and then he stopped. He couldn't hear Corb and could see the window in the end of the corridor ahead of him framing a segment of the lighter night sky. Had Corb gone into a room?

Even while he was watching, listening to a woman run down the corridor behind him, he saw a ladder drop down across the window and the form of Corb climbing it.

He shot once, heard a bitter oath and then ran for the

ladder. As he reached it he saw it being pulled up by a rope from the roof, and he leaped for it. His hands caught the bottom rung, and his weight suddenly broke Corb's hold on the rope. The ladder crashed to the floor and Frank with it. He hit the floor and rolled just as Corb shot down into the corridor. Frank palmed up his other gun and set three fast shots at the trap-door hole, then came to his feet and climbed the ladder, shooting his gun empty. He didn't know whether or not Corb was waiting up there to get him, but he had to take the chance. He raced up the ladder, hurled himself through the square hole and fell on the roof, rolling over and over down its slope. A fusillade of shots seemed to follow his course until he was brought up against a chimney. He rolled behind it, then feverishly started to reload his guns, peering out from behind the chimney. He saw another chimney beyond the trap door, and this was where Corb was forted up.

Frank swung his loading gates shut and then heard the shooting below. Some of it came from the front stairway and some seemed to be coming from the back part of the hotel. In a few moments they would be up after him. He peered out from behind the chimney and took stock of the situation. Then he called, "Here I come, Corb."

No answer.

The roof was almost flat, sloping toward the rear, and Corb was upslope from him. Again, as in the store, there was the light behind Corb and darkness behind him. Corb couldn't see him well, and Frank decided to take the chance. He broke out from behind the chimney, quartering away from Corb, holding his fire and running. Corb opened up, but he was shooting blindly toward the chimney. Frank ran to one side until he saw Corb's figure crouched behind the chimney, and then he opened up with both guns.

Corb grunted and came to his feet, and Frank knew he was hit. Then Corb, firing as he ran, headed up the roof in a panic to get away from Frank. He was limping, bent over so low that he was behind the dark line of the wooden parapet at the front of the building, and Frank could not see him.

He ran anyway, shooting blindly at the noise Corb's dragging feet made. And then the noise ceased, and Frank could see nothing. He dropped on his belly and started crawling up the slope, a gun in each hand. Corb was hiding somewhere behind the parapet, Frank knew.

Suddenly something loomed up in front of Frank. It was a low brick ventilator. Then, confident of his shelter, Frank opened up. He trained his gun in a line with the parapet and, spacing his shots, he opened up in a sustained roar of gunfire.

Suddenly there was a scream, and Frank saw Corb's body rise up full height, clutching his chest. Frank shot then, blindly and furiously, and he saw Corb driven back until his back, acting as a pivot, bent over the parapet. Then slowly, almost gracefully, he toppled over and disappeared. Frank rose and ran the ten yards to the parapet. Before he reached it he heard a great rending crash of splitting wood. When he got to the parapet he looked over. He saw, a story and a half below him, a jagged hole in the boards of the wooden awning, and he straightened up, a little sick, just as a soldier's voice called from the trap door: "Raise 'em high, cowboy, or you're dead!"

Chapter XX

FRANK WAS MARCHED DOWNSTAIRS between a squad of soldiers to the porch. Someone already had thrown a canvas over Corb's broken body, and Major Corning, surrounded by his officers, was standing under the street lamp. Red, surly and disarmed, and Luvie and Edith and Otey, his gun rammed in the back of two of Corb's men, were waiting with Major Corning.

Frank walked wearily over to them, and Major Corning said grimly, "This time you won't escape, Christian."

It brought a laugh from the crowd gathered behind the soldiers who ringed the group.

"Escape?" Luvie said indignantly. "Why should he? He's not guilty of anything."

Major Corning turned to her. "For a lady who held off my troopers with ten minutes of gunfire, you haven't exactly the right to speak."

"Then I have," a voice said from the crowd. Chet Milabel shouldered his way through the soldiers. "I'm askin' why he should be arrested."

"You just saw a murder!" Major Corning said.

"Like hell I did," Milabel said roughly. "I saw justice.

Corb killed this man's partner. He's got the proof if you'll listen to him."

"I'll listen," the major said, turning to Frank. "What proof have you that Corb killed Wheelon?"

Frank warily produced the pair of spurs and the rowel and told his story briefly. Milabel backed him up. Luvie and Red and Otey and Barnes, who had drawn closer now, verified the story Gus had told at the camp. At the storm of talk that poured from them all Major Corning raised his hands to his ears.

"All right, all right!" he said angrily. "Perhaps that's so. Still, there's a 'dead or alive' reward on Christian's head for murdering a trail driver of Milabel's. And you preferred the charges yourself, along with Corb!" he said to Milabel.

Otey said harshly, "Red, take this gun and keep these two jaspers here! Major, keep your mouth shut until I get back!"

The major glared at him, but Otey vanished into the night. In two minutes he led a staggering Beach Freeman out of the compound into the circle of lamplight. Beach's face was a bloody pulp, and Otey had to hold him upright.

Otey stood him up in front of Major Corning and said, "Beach, who killed that rider of Milabel's at the stampede? Talk straight, or you'll get more of what you've already got."

"I did," Beach whined through puffed lips. "It—it was a mistake," he said weakly. "I had to."

"And I fired him for it," Frank said angrily to the major.

Milabel looked over at Frank. "I'm glad to hear that," he said softly. "Damned if I ever thought you did it." He looked at Major Corning. "What else have you got against him, Major?"

Major Corning's voice was sharp with anger. "What else? I understand from talk around here that Christian killed four of Corb's riders in a night attack."

Red raised his foot and savagely kicked the two Corb understrappers before the major. "You gents aim to talk, or will I turn you over to the major as whisky peddlers?" Red drawled. "Gus told me your caches. I know every one of 'em."

One rider glared at Red, then said sullenly to the major, "I was on that raid. Corb raided Christian, not the other way. We got what we had comin' to us, I reckon."

Major Corning's mouth was agape. He looked at his officers, and they could only look at him mutely.

Frank said calmly, "What else is in the list, Major?"

"Escaping from our soldiers," Major Corning stammered.

"Stone Bull rescued him," Edith put in. "Take it up with him. Frank had nothing to do with it."

A captain spoke up. "There's a little matter of whisky peddling, Major. That was the cause of the original arrest."

"And I framed it on Christian," Milabel countered. "I stole the whisky from Corb's cache and planted it on Frank's range."

Major Corning said furiously, "For a man who has been feuding with Christian ever since he got here, you seem mighty interested in having him set free, Milabel!"

"I am," Milabel said, his broad face cracking into a grin. "He's made me eat every word I ever bragged. I want him for a neighbor."

"Still, he broke jail," the captain put in.

"But it was a false charge," Frank countered.

Luvie walked up to Major Corning and faced him. "Major Corning, you've had the biggest menace on this reservation wiped out tonight. The biggest whisky peddler, a renegade Indian leader and a cattle rustler. And you want the man jailed who did it. That may sound like the United States Army to some people, but it's not my army. Is it yours?"

Major Corning looked searchingly at her, and then he said gently, "No, my dear, it's not. But argument can bring out lots besides tears. Tonight it's brought out the truth." He walked over to Frank and put out his hand. "You're free as air, as far as I'm concerned, son. All I'll burden you with is my heartfelt thanks."

Frank took his hand and a slow smile broke over his tired face. Before he had time to thank the major a cavalry officer rode up, and the crowd broke for him. He saluted and said, "All the leaders are in the guardhouse, Major, and Captain Brett has returned safely from the Indian camp."

"Is it over?" Major Corning asked.

The officer smiled faintly. "I don't know, sir, but the drums have stopped beating."

Major Corning looked at Red, then walked over to him. He put out his hand again, and he said, "It's a pity you aren't an army man, Shibe. You could use a little discipline—but that's all you could use. Thanks for what you've done. And in case there's any doubt about it, you have the run of this garrison from now to eternity, with a standing invitation to eat in the officers' mess as long as I'm in command."

He saluted Edith and Luvie and marched off across the

parade grounds, and his officers behind him. The troops were ordered to fall in and marched off, and slowly the crowd broke up.

Red found Edith standing beside him. "It kind of pays off for Morg's murder, don't it?" he murmured.

Edith nodded, and a shadow crossed her face. But only for a moment, and then she smiled at Red. "Morg was lucky to have the friends he had, Red."

"Frank will do to ride the river with," Red said gently.

Edith looked up at him. "He will. But Morg had another friend that will do to ride the river with too."

Red looked down at her, and his freckled face was suddenly close to the color of his hair. "I ain't ever been tagged with that," he stammered.

Edith smiled a little and put her hand through his arm. "Then maybe you'd better get used to it, Red, because I think so."

Luvie watched Frank put the spurs in his hip pocket and wipe his forehead, and then she turned to her father. "Come on, Dad," she said miserably.

She put a hand through her father's arm and then started for the hotel.

She heard footsteps behind her, and Frank swung in alongside them.

"You think you'd trust Luvie to walk around the parade grounds with me, Mr. Barnes?" he asked.

Barnes laughed and said, "Let her answer that, Frank."

"Good night, Dad," Luvie murmured.

She and Frank started out across the parade grounds, heading instinctively for a spot where the street lamps were not so bright.

Frank didn't say anything for a long time, until they were in the shaded street where the married officers' quarters were.

Suddenly he said, "Major Corning said somethin' there tonight I didn't rightly understand."

"What was that?"

"He said you held off the troopers with a gun." He looked sideways at her. "Did you?"

"Yes," Luvie said softly.

"But—why?"

"I owed it to you," Luvie said, and then her voice was gentle with quiet pride. "You didn't believe me when I said I was sorry, Frank. I—I had to show you the only way I could."

Frank didn't speak for a moment, and then he said, "I reckon I see," and there was disappointment in his voice.

"No, you don't, Frank," Luvie said. They stopped and faced each other. "Frank, are you going to make me say it?"

"Wait a minute, Luvie," Frank said huskily. "I'm takin' a chance on what you mean, and I'm goin' to say it. You've been my woman ever since I saw you, fightin' or no fightin', and you can go away and I'll never see you again and you'll still be my woman. Mine! Do you understand?"

"Understand?" Luvie echoed. She laughed shakily. "It's what I've known before you knew it, Frank."

And Frank took her in his arms and held her close to him, knowing they had both been fools and a little glad of it and not caring.

When, hand in hand, they came back to the hotel much later Otey and Milabel were seated on the porch steps under the light.

At their approach Otey said truculently, "Frank, make this damn jughead see sense. We can't put out no five men on a roundup wagon to separate our herds!"

Milabel laughed and said, "Listen, runt. You can if I loan you the five men, can't you?"

ABOUT THE AUTHOR

LUKE SHORT, whose real name was Frederick D. Glidden, was born in Illinois in 1907. He wrote nearly fifty books about the West and was a winner of the special Western Heritage Trustee Award. Before devoting himself to writing westerns, he was a trapper in the Canadian Sub-arctic, worked as an assistant to an archeologist, and was a newsman. Luke Short believed an author could write best about the places he knows most intimately, so he usually located his westerns on familiar ground. Luke Short died in 1975.

"REACH FOR THE SKY!"

and you still won't find more excitement or more thrills than you get in Bantam's slam-bang, action-packed westerns! Here's a roundup of fast-reading stories by some of America's greatest western writers:

☐ 14823	**THE PROVING TRAIL** Louis L'Amour		$1.95
☐ 13651	**THE STRONG SHALL LIVE**		$1.95
☐ 13781	**THE IRON MARSHAL**		$1.95
☐ 14219	**OVER ON THE DRY SIDE** Louis L'Armour		$1.95
☐ 13719	**RADIGAN** Louis L'Amour		$1.95
☐ 14207	**THE WARRIOR'S PATH** Louis L'Amour		$1.95
☐ 12378	**THE WHIP** Luke Short		$1.50
☐ 13759	**THE TOUGH TEXAN** Will Cook		$1.75
☐ 12888	**GUNSIGHTS** Elmore Leonard		$1.50
☐ 14176	**FEUD AT SINGLE SHOT** Luke Short		$1.75
☐ 14236	**THE BEAR PAW HORSES** Will Henry		$1.75
☐ 12374	**ROYAL GORGE** Pete Dawson		$1.50
☐ 13923	**GUNMAN BRAND** Thomas Thompson		$1.50
☐ 08773	**THIS GUN IS STILL** Frank Gruber		$1.50
☐ 12978	**WARBONNET** Clay Fisher		$1.50

Buy them at your local bookstore or use this handy coupon for ordering: